"Tell me something about me," she said, apprehension fluttering inside her belly along with the first swirling current of doubt. **"Tell me something no one else knows."**

"You were a virgin."

She stamped down on the blush that threatened. Was a virgin? "That wouldn't have been a secret. Tell me something I might have told you, something personal."

He flung his hands wide in exasperation. "Such as? You weren't very talkative, Isabella. I believe you once said that your single goal in life was to please me."

"That's ridiculous," she answered, her voice little more than a whisper. Because she had been raised to please a man, to be the perfect wife, and it was exactly the sort of thing she would have been expected to say. But to actually have said it? To this man?

He gazed  rk eyes settling o̶ had a picture i̶ he image was shock̶ her it was a me̶

All about the author...
Lynn Raye Harris

LYNN RAYE HARRIS read her first Harlequin romance
novel when her grandmother carted home a box from a yard
sale. She didn't know she wanted to be a writer then, but she
definitely knew she wanted to marry a sheikh or a prince and
live the glamorous life she read about in the pages. Instead, she
married a military man and moved around the world. She's
been inside the Kremlin, hiked up a Korean mountain, floated
on a gondola in Venice and stood inside volcanoes at opposite
ends of the world.

These days Lynn lives in North Alabama with her handsome
husband and two crazy cats. When she's not writing, she loves
to read, shop for antiques, cook gourmet meals and try new
wines. She is also an avowed shoeaholic and thinks there's
nothing better than a new pair of high heels.

Lynn was a finalist in the 2008 Romance Writers of America's
Golden Heart® contest, and she is the winner of the
Harlequin® Presents Instant Seduction contest. She loves a
hot hero, a heroine with attitude and a happy ending. Writing
passionate stories for Harlequin Books is a dream come true.
You can visit her at www.lynnrayeharris.com.

Lynn Raye Harris

STRANGERS IN THE DESERT

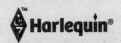

TORONTO NEW YORK LONDON
AMSTERDAM PARIS SYDNEY HAMBURG
STOCKHOLM ATHENS TOKYO MILAN MADRID
PRAGUE WARSAW BUDAPEST AUCKLAND

Recycling programs
for this product may
not exist in your area.

ISBN-13: 978-0-373-13057-3

STRANGERS IN THE DESERT

First North American Publication 2012

STRANGERS IN THE DESERT

In memory of Sally Jo Harris, beloved aunt-in-law, intrepid adventurer and amazing human being. I can't believe I will never get to talk about books, travel, great coffee and fabulous food with you ever again. You brought joy wherever you went, and you left us too suddenly. We miss you.

CHAPTER ONE

"...THE possibility she is still alive."

Adan looked up from the papers his secretary had given him to sign. He'd been only half paying attention to the functionary who'd been speaking. Since his uncle had died a week ago, there'd been so much to do in preparation for his own coronation that he often did as many things at once as he could. "Repeat that," he ordered, every cell of his body revving into high alert.

The man who stood inside the door trembled as Adan focused on him. He bowed his head and spoke to the floor.

"Forgive me, Your Excellency. I said that in preparation for your upcoming nuptials to Jasmine Shadi, we must investigate all reports that reach us in regards to your late wife, since her body was never recovered."

"It was never recovered because she walked into the desert, Hakim," Adan said mildly, though irritation spiked within him. "Isabella is buried under an ocean of sand."

As always, he felt a pang of sadness for his son. Though Adan had lost a wife, it was the fact Rafiq had lost his mother that bothered Adan most. Theirs had been an arranged marriage, not a love match. While he hoped that Isabella had not suffered, he could drag up very little emotion for her.

Isabella Maro had been beautiful, but she'd been unremarkable in every other way. Quiet, lovely and well-suited to performing the duties of their station, she'd been exactly what his wife should have been. And though he hadn't been the heir to the throne then, he had no doubt she'd have made a lovely queen.

A lovely, bland queen.

It wasn't her fault. Though she had been half-American, she'd been raised by her father as a traditional Jahfaran woman. He would never forget that when he'd met her shortly before their wedding, he'd asked her what she wanted out of life. She'd told him that she wanted whatever he wanted.

"There has been a reported sighting, Your Excellency."

Adan gripped the pen he'd been signing papers with and spread his other hand flat on the desk. He needed something solid to hold on to. Something to remind him that he wasn't in the middle of a nightmare. In order to ascend the throne formally, he needed a wife. Jasmine Shadi was to be that wife, and he was marrying her in two weeks time. There was no place in his life for a phantom.

"A *sighting,* Hakim?"

Hakim swallowed. His nut-brown skin glistened with moisture, though the palace had been modernized years ago and the air conditioners seemed to be working fine.

"Sharif Al Omar—a business competitor of Hassan Maro's, Your Excellency—recently returned from a trip to the island of Maui. He says there was a singer in a bar there, a woman who called herself Bella Tyler, who resembled your late wife, sire."

"A singer in a bar?" Adan stared at the man a full minute before he burst into laughter. Isabella had survived the desert and now sang in a bar on a remote Hawaiian island? Impossible. No one ever survived the burning Jahfaran desert if they weren't prepared.

And Isabella had not been prepared. She'd wandered alone into the deepest wastes of Jahfar. At night. A sandstorm the next day had obliterated every trace of her, though they'd looked for weeks. "Hakim, I think Mr. Al Omar needs to see a doctor. Clearly, Hawaiian sunshine is somehow more brutal than our Jahfaran sun."

"He took a picture, sire."

Adan stilled. "Do you have this picture?"

"I do, sire." The man held out a folder. Mahmoud, his secretary, took the file and set it on the desk in front of Adan. He hesitated only a moment before flipping open the cover. Adan stared at the picture for so long that the lines started to blur. It could not be her, and yet…

"Cancel all my appointments for the next three days," he finally said. "And call the airport to ready my plane."

The bar was crowded tonight. Tourists and locals alike jammed into the interior and spilled out the open walls onto the beach below. The sun had just started to dip into the ocean, and the sky was turning brilliant gold when Isabella walked onto the stage and took her place behind the microphone. The sun sank fast—much faster than she'd ever believed possible when she'd first arrived on the island—and then it was gone and the sky was pink, the clouds high over the ocean tinged purple and red with the last rays.

It was a brilliant and beautiful sight, and it always made her heart ache and seem full all at once. She'd grown accustomed to the melancholy, though she did not know from where it sprang. She often felt as if a piece of her was missing, but she didn't know what that piece was.

Singing filled the void, for a brief time anyway.

Isabella looked out at the gathered crowd. They were waiting for *her*. They were here for her. She closed her eyes and began to sing, losing herself in the rhythm and feel of the music. On the stage, she was Bella Tyler—and Bella was completely in control of herself and her life.

Unlike Isabella Maro.

She slid from one song into the next, her voice wrapping around the words, caressing them. The lights were hot, but she was used to the heat. She wore a bikini and a sarong for island flavor, though she did not sing many island songs. Her eyelids felt weighted down beneath the makeup she wore. She always applied it thickly for the stage, or it wouldn't show up in the bright lights. Around her neck she wore a white puka-shell necklace. A matching bracelet encircled one ankle.

Her hair had grown and was no longer twined in the sleek knot she'd once favored. It was heavier, blonder and wild with seawater and sunshine. Her father would be horrified, no doubt, not only at the hair but also at the immodesty of her dress. She smiled into the microphone, thinking of his reaction. A man in the front smiled back, mistaking the gesture. She didn't mind; it was part of the act, part of the personality of Bella Tyler.

Except that Bella wouldn't go home with this man. Or any man. It didn't feel right somehow. Had never felt right since the moment she'd come to the States. She was free now, free from the expectations and duty her father had raised her with, and yet she couldn't shake the idea she had to save herself for someone.

"Bella Tyler, ladies and gentlemen," the guitarist announced when she finished the last song. The bar erupted in applause.

"Mahalo," Isabella said as she shoved a strand of damp hair behind her ear. "And now we're going to take a little break. We'll be back in fifteen."

As she left the stage, she grabbed the glass of water that Grant, the club manager, held out for her, and headed into the back for a few minutes' rest. The room she went to could hardly be called a dressing room, and yet it was where she stowed her stuff and applied her makeup for the evening. She flopped onto a chair and propped her bare feet on a bamboo trunk that served as a coffee table.

Laughter and disembodied voices from the beach came to her through the thin walls. The rest of the band would work their way back here eventually, if they didn't grab a cigarette and head outside to smoke instead. Isabella tilted her head back and touched the icy glass to her collarbone. The coldness of it was a pleasant shock as moisture dripped between her breasts.

A few moments later, she heard movement in the hall. She could sense the moment when someone stopped in the doorway. The room was small, and she could feel that she was no longer alone. But people were always coming and going in Ka Nui's, so she didn't open her eyes to see who it was.

But it wasn't a waitress grabbing something, or one of the band members come to join her, because the person hadn't moved since she'd first sensed a presence.

But was the visitor still there—or was she imagining things?

Isabella's eyes snapped open. A man stood in the entry, his presence dark and overwhelming. Raw panic seized her throat tight so that she couldn't speak or cry out. At first, all she saw was his size—he was tall and broad and filled the door—but then she began to pick out individual features.

A shiver slid down her backbone as she realized with a jolt that he was Jahfaran. Dark hair, piercing dark eyes and skin that had been burnished by the powerful desert sun. Though he was dressed in a navy blue shirt and khaki pants instead of a *dishdasha,* he had the look of the desert, that hawklike intensity of a man who lived life on the edge of civilization. She didn't know why, but fear flooded her in waves, liquefying her bones until she couldn't move.

"You will tell me," he said tightly, *"why."*

Isabella blinked. "Why?" she repeated. Somehow, she managed to scramble to her feet. He was so tall that she still had to tilt her head back to look up at him. Her heart thundered in her breast as she realized he was terribly, frighteningly angry.

With her.

His gaze skimmed down her body. When his eyes met hers again, they burned with disgust. "Look at you," he said. "You look like a prostitute."

The cold fear that had pooled in her stomach began to boil as anger stirred within. How typical of a Jahfaran male. How absolutely typical to think he had a right to criticize her simply because she was female, and because he did not understand her choices.

Isabella drew herself up. She thrust her chin out, propped her hands on her hips and gave him the same thorough once-over he'd given her. It was bold, but she didn't care. She owed this man nothing.

"I don't know who you think you are, but you're welcome to get the hell out of my dressing room and keep your opinions to yourself."

His expression grew lethally cold. "Don't play games with me, Isabella."

She took a step back, her pulse thrumming in her throat at breakneck speed. He'd used her name—her given name—and it stunned her, though perhaps it should not have. Clearly, he knew her father, and he'd recognized her somehow. Perhaps they'd met in the course of her father's business dealings. A party, a dinner...

But no. She didn't recognize him. And she was sure that she'd never have forgotten a man like this if she'd met him. He was too big, too magnificent—and much too full of himself. He would have been impossible to ignore.

"Why would I play games with you? I don't even know you!"

His eyes narrowed. "I will know how you came to be here, and I will know it *now*."

Isabella drew herself up. How dare he question her as if he had a right? "You're bright. Figure it out."

He took a step into the room, and the room shrank. He overwhelmed the space. He overwhelmed her.

Isabella wanted to back away from him, but there was nowhere to go. And she would not cower before this man. It seemed vitally important somehow that she did not.

"You did not do this alone," he said. "Who helped you?"

Isabella swallowed. "I—"

"Is everything okay here, Bella?"

Her eyes darted past the stranger to Grant, who stood in the door, his fists clenched at his sides. The stranger had turned at his entrance. Grant's expression was grave, his blue eyes deadly serious as he tried to stare the man down.

She could have told him it wouldn't work. The man stared back at Grant, his expression not softening in the least. The last thing she wanted was a fight, because she did not doubt that Grant would try to defend her. She also didn't doubt that he would lose. There was something hard and cold about this man. Something fierce and untamed.

"I'm fine, Grant," she said. "Mr...um, the gentleman was just leaving."

"I was not, in fact," he said, his English oh-so-perfect. The cultured tone of his voice proclaimed him to be from an elite family, the ones who usually sent their sons to be schooled in the United Kingdom.

"I think you should go," Grant said. "Bella needs to rest before she goes back on."

"Indeed." The stranger turned back to her then, and she felt the full force of his laserlike attention. "Sadly, she will not be returning to the stage. Isabella is coming with me."

Fury pounded through her. "I am *not*—"

He reached out and grasped her arm with an iron fist.

His fingers didn't bite into her, but they were firm and in control. Commanding.

Shock forced Isabella to go completely still as her body reacted with a shudder at the touch of his skin on hers.

But it wasn't revulsion she felt. It wasn't terror.

It was familiarity. It was heat and want and, underlying that, a current of sadness so deep and strong she wanted to sob.

It stunned her into immobility as she tried to process it.

Why?

"Hey," Grant protested. "Let her go!"

At the same time, Isabella looked up in confusion. "Who *are* you?"

A shadow passed over his face before it hardened again. "Do you really expect me to believe you do not know?"

Anger and despair slashed through her in waves. It made no sense. And yet he hated her. This man *hated* her, and she had no idea why. Somehow, she found the strength to act, wrenching herself free from his grip.

Isabella hugged her arms around her torso as if to shield herself. She couldn't bear to feel the anger and sadness ripping through her a moment longer. Couldn't bear the currents of heat arcing across her nerve endings. The swirling confusion. The crushing desperation.

Grant had disappeared, but she knew it was so he could fetch one of the bouncers. He'd be back at any moment, and this man would be thrown out on his arrogant behind. She was going to enjoy that.

"Of course I don't know you," she snapped.

"On the contrary," he growled, his dark eyes flashing hot, "you know me *very* well."

Her heart pounded at the certainty in his voice. He was insane. Gorgeous, but insane. "I can't imagine why you would think so."

"Because," he replied, his voice laced with barely contained rage, "you are my *wife*."

CHAPTER TWO

SHE gaped at him like a fish. There was no other way to describe it. If he didn't know better, he'd think she truly was shocked. Adan's mouth twisted. Who'd have thought that little Isabella Maro was such a fine actress? He'd had no idea, or he'd have paid her much closer attention.

Because, clearly, she'd duped him. Duped them all.

And he was going to find out why.

She hadn't acted alone, of that he was certain. Had she had a lover who'd helped her to escape?

The thought lodged in his gut like a shard of ice.

What a cold, cruel woman she was. She'd abandoned her baby son, left him to grow up motherless. She'd cared more for herself than she had for Rafiq.

Adan hated her for it.

And he hated this stirring in his blood as he looked at her. It was anger, yes, but it was something more, as well. His gaze slid over her nearly naked body. She was wearing a red bikini with a tropical-print sarong tied over one hip. Her nipples jutted through the meager fabric of her top, drawing his attention. He remembered, though he did not wish to, the creamy beauty of her breasts, the large pink areolas, the tightly budded nipples in their center. He remembered her shyness the first time they'd made love, the way she'd quickly adapted to him, the way she'd welcomed him into her bed for an entire month of passionate nights.

He'd stopped going to her bed because she'd fallen pregnant. Not because he had wanted to, but because she'd become so sick that lovemaking was out of the question.

"Your wife?" She shook her head adamantly. "You're mistaken."

Behind him, he heard the heavy stomp of footsteps. And then the man she'd called Grant—the man who'd looked at her with his heart in his eyes—was back, a large Samoan by his side.

"I'll ask you once more to leave," Grant said. "Makuna will escort you out."

Adan gave them his most quelling look. He had a six-man security team outside. Not because he'd expected trouble, but because he was a head of state and didn't travel without security. One signal to them, and they would storm this place with guns drawn.

It wasn't something he wanted to do, and yet he wasn't leaving without Isabella. Without his wife.

"It's okay, Grant," he heard her say behind him. "I'll talk to him for a few minutes."

Grant looked confused. But then he nodded once and tapped Makuna on the arm. The two of them melted away from the door, and Adan was once more alone with Isabella.

"Wise decision," he said.

She sank onto the chair she'd originally been sitting in. Her fingers trembled as they shoved her riot of dark golden hair from her face. Her heavily made-up eyes stared at him in confusion.

"Why would you think I'm your wife? I've never been married."

Anger clawed at his insides. "Deny it all you like, but it won't make it any less true."

Her brows drew down as she stared at him. "I don't know why you're telling me this, or why you think I'm your wife. I've never met you. I don't even know your name."

He didn't believe it for a moment. "Adan," he said, because arguing about it was pointless when she insisted on carrying through with her fiction.

"Adan," she repeated. "I left Jahfar a long time ago. I think I'd remember a husband."

"I won't play this game with you, Isabella," he growled. "Do you really expect me to believe you don't remember? How stupid do you think I am?"

She frowned deeply. "I never said that. I said I didn't know you. I think you've confused me with someone else. It's not unusual for men to try and get close to me in this business. They see me sing and they think I'm available for an easy hookup. But I'm not, okay?"

Adan wanted to shake her. "You are Isabella Maro, daughter of Hassan Maro and an American woman, Beth Tyler. Nearly three years ago, you and I were wed. Two years ago, you walked into the desert and were never seen again."

He couldn't bring himself to mention Rafiq to her, not when she was so obviously trying to play him for a fool.

She blinked, her expression going carefully blank. And then she shook her head. "No, I…"

"What?" he prompted when she didn't continue.

She swallowed. "I had an accident, it's true. But I've recovered." Her fingers lifted to press against her lips. He noticed they were trembling. "There are things that are fuzzy, but—" She shook her head. "No, someone would have told me."

Everything inside him went still. "Someone? Who would have told you, Isabella? Who knows you are here?"

She met his gaze again. "My parents, of course. My father sent me to my mother's to recover. The doctor said I needed to get away from Jahfar, that it was too hot, too…stressful."

Fury whipped through him. And disbelief. Her parents knew she was alive? Impossible.

And yet, he'd hardly seen Hassan Maro since Isabella had disappeared. The man spent more time out of the country these days than he did in it. Adan had chalked it up to his business interests and to grief over the loss of his only daughter, but what if it were more? What if Maro were hiding something?

Was the man truly capable of helping his daughter to escape her marriage when he'd been so thrilled with the arrangement in the first place?

Adan shook his head. She was lying, playing him, denying what she knew to be true simply because she'd been caught. She'd survived the desert, there was no doubt, and she could not have done so without help.

But whose help?

"I have never heard of selective amnesia, Isabella," he growled. "How could you remember your parents, remember Jahfar—yet not remember me?"

"I didn't say I had amnesia!" she cried. "You did."

"What do you call it, then, if you say you know who you are and where you come from, but you can't remember the husband you left behind?"

"We're not married," she insisted—and yet her lower lip trembled. It was the first sign of a small chink in her armor, as if she knew she'd been caught and was desperate to escape.

Adan hardened his resolve. She would not do so, not until he was finished with her. She had much to answer for. And much still to pay for.

She clasped her hands in front of her body. The motion pressed her breasts together, emphasized the smooth, plump curves. A tingle started at the base of his spine and drifted outward.

No.

Adan ruthlessly clamped down on his libido. Was he so shallow as to allow the sight of a woman's half-naked body to arouse him, when the woman was as treacherous as this one? When he had every reason to despise her?

"Let's turn this around, then," she said, worrying her bottom lip with her teeth. "Assuming for a moment that you're correct, that we *are* married—where have you been and why didn't you come for me sooner?"

"I have been in Jahfar," he ground out. "And, as you very well know, I believed you to be dead."

Her face grew pale beneath her tan. "Dead?"

He was tired of this, tired of the caginess and obfuscation. He'd flown through several time zones and had had no sleep in his quest to learn if the picture were true, if the woman holding a microphone and peering up at the camera as if to a secret lover was indeed his wife. He'd told himself it wasn't possible. She could not have survived.

But then he'd walked into this bar and seen her standing there, her face so familiar and so strange all at once, and he'd known the truth.

And he was done being civil. "You walked into the *desert,* Isabella. What you did after that is anyone's guess, but you did not come back out. We searched for weeks."

She shook her head. "It's insane, absolutely insane."

"Is it?" Adan tucked his hand under her elbow and pulled her out of the chair. She rose surprisingly easily, as if she were distracted. He pointedly ignored the current of electricity that zapped through him when he touched her bare skin.

She looked up at him, her dark, smoky eyes full of emotion. "I don't remember."

He would not be moved. "Gather your things. We're leaving."

Married.

Isabella shook her head. It was impossible. But a knot of fear lodged in her stomach like a lump of ice. She had a few fuzzy spots in her memory, it was true, and yet, how could this man be a part of it? How could she possibly forget something as *monumental* as a husband?

She could not. It was out of the question. Besides, her parents would not have kept this from her. Why would they do so? What terrible thing would make them do so?

There was one way to clear this up. Isabella turned and grabbed her purse, digging through it for her cell phone.

"What are you doing?" Adan asked.

She whipped the phone out and held it up triumphantly.

Her hair was in her eyes, stuck to the lipstick on her mouth, but she didn't care. She knew she looked wild. She felt wild.

Crazy.

He'd said she was dead—that everyone in Jahfar believed she was dead.

But her father knew she wasn't, so how could that be?

When she'd asked questions about her accident, he'd told her it was better if she did not know the specifics. She'd been in a wreck, and she'd fallen into a coma. There were drugs, pain meds, and they were making her memory fuzzy. It was nothing, he'd insisted.

Nothing.

Her mother, typically, hadn't known anything about what Isabella's life in Jahfar had been like. Beth Tyler had been gone from the country for ten years, and though she'd seemed pleased when Isabella came to stay with her, they'd both been a little relieved when Isabella had moved on.

But if she'd been married, wouldn't her mother have known about it? Wouldn't she have attended the wedding?

Now, Isabella looked up, into the hard, handsome face of the man standing so near. He didn't look like *nothing* to her. Isabella gave her head a little shake. No, her parents would *not* have lied about this. There was no reason for it!

"I'm calling my father," she said as she began to scroll through the phone's contacts. "He'll know the truth."

Adan stiffened as if she'd slapped him. "Do you

mean to tell me that your father really does know you're here?"

Isabella frowned. "I already said so, didn't I?"

He swore in Arabic, a vile curse that shocked her with its vehemence and profanity. She'd been in the States for more than a year now—was it closer to two?—and she'd heard a lot of foul language. But she wasn't accustomed to hearing it in Arabic. In Jahfar, she'd been cosseted and protected—a lady who had been bred to marry a powerful sheikh someday.

Until her accident changed everything.

He grabbed the phone out of her hand. "You will not call him."

Isabella reached for the phone, but he held it just out of range. She folded her arms and glared at him. She should be relieved. "Then I guess you're lying to me about being married. Because my father could expose the lie, right?"

"If it amuses you to think it, by all means do so." He tucked the phone into his breast pocket. She tried not to let her gaze stray to the hard muscle exposed by the open V of his shirt. If she'd seen him on the beach, she'd have thought he was magnificent. No doubt about it.

But he was hard and cold, and she had no business finding him attractive. Not to mention, he was lying.

"If that's not what you're worried about, then why can't I call him?" she challenged.

"Because I intend to deal with him myself, when we return to Jahfar."

Isabella's blood ran cold for reasons she couldn't begin to articulate. Jahfar. The desert. The hard, harsh landscape of her father's heritage. It was her heritage, too, and yet there was something primitive about it that she couldn't quite make her peace with. The idea of going back caused a wave of panic to rise like bile in her throat.

"I'm not going with you."

His dark eyes slid down her body, back up again. "And just how do you propose to stop me from taking you, Isabella?"

"I'll scream," she said, her heart thudding a million miles an hour.

"Will you now?" He was so cool, so smug, that a knot of fear gathered in her stomach and refused to let go. He would throw her over his shoulder and haul her bodily out of here. He was big enough and bold enough to do it.

"They won't let you take me. My friends will help," she said with as much bravado as she could muster.

His laugh was not in the least bit amused. "They are welcome to try. But Isabella, I have my own personal security. If anyone touches me, they will assume it is an assassination attempt. I cannot be responsible for the measures they might take."

Ice coated the chambers of her heart. He was every bit as cold and cruel as he seemed. And she had no doubt he would take delight in hurting anyone who attempted to stop him.

"It's no wonder I can't remember you," she said bitterly. "You're a tyrant. Being married to you would be hell on earth, I'm sure. Any woman would do better walking into the desert to die than staying with you."

The corners of his mouth tightened. "Would to God that you had truly done so and saved me the trouble of dealing with you now."

She couldn't say why, but her heart constricted. Why

did she care? He meant nothing to her. She didn't even like him.

"*If* we are married, then why don't you save us both a lot of trouble and divorce me? You're a Jahfaran male. The power is yours," she said as coldly as she could.

Would to God that you had truly done so and saved me the trouble...

His cruel words echoed in her head. She meant nothing to him. She was a problem, an embarrassment. An issue to be dealt with.

It was too much like her childhood, when she'd felt like an object that her parents fought over after the divorce. An issue they would never solve. She'd tried to be good, tried to be so good and perfect for them both. But she could not please them, no matter how she tried.

Isabella swallowed angry tears. She was finished with trying to please anyone but herself.

"If only it were that easy," he growled. "But circumstances have changed, and we must return to Jahfar."

"You can't simply expect me to leave with you when you've given me no proof. To me, you're a stranger. I don't know you, and I'm not going anywhere with you."

His eyes hardened. "What proof would you have me give you? Shall I tell you that we met only a week before we married, and that you were as frightened and meek as a lamb? Or perhaps you'd like to hear that the wedding feast went on for three days and cost in excess of a half-million American dollars? Or that your father was supremely pleased that he'd managed to wed you to a prince?"

Isabella's stomach went into a free fall. "A prince? You're a prince?"

"I was," he said, and though she didn't know what he meant by that, she didn't ask.

She wiped damp palms across her sarong. It simply couldn't be true. Status was everything in Jahfar. If her father had managed to arrange a marriage with the royal family, he'd have been so proud. He would not have lied about it.

"Tell me something about me," she said, apprehension fluttering inside her belly along with the first swirling current of doubt. "Tell me something no one else knows."

"You were a virgin."

She stamped down on the blush that threatened. *Was* a virgin? "That wouldn't have been a secret. Tell me something I might have told you, something personal."

He flung his hands wide in exasperation. "Such as? You weren't very talkative, Isabella. I believe you once said that your single goal in life was to please *me*."

"That's ridiculous," she answered, her voice little more than a whisper. Because she *had* been raised to please a man, to be the perfect wife, and it was exactly the sort of thing she would have been expected to say. But to actually have said it? To *this* man?

"Enough," he said, slashing a hand in the air before reaching into his khakis and pulling out a cell phone. "We are leaving."

"Wait just a damn minute," Isabella cried, closing the distance between them and grabbing his wrist before he punched the buttons. He wasn't *listening* to her, and she wasn't about to meekly accept his decree.

Heat sizzled into her where she gripped him. So much heat. Her fingers couldn't span his wrist.

He gazed down at her with glittering dark eyes. His

sensual mouth was flat, hard. She wondered what he looked like when he smiled. Black stubble shadowed his jaw, so sexy and alluring that she wanted to reach up and feel the roughness against her palm.

His gaze settled on her mouth, and she suddenly had a picture in her head of him kissing her. The image was shocking. And she didn't know whether it was a memory or a desire.

Yet her body responded to the very real longing it called up, softening, melting, aching. The moment spun out between them until she felt as if they must have been standing this way for hours.

He swore softly in Arabic, and then he broke her grip on his wrist and tangled both his hands in her hair. Something dropped and hit the woven rug beneath their feet. Her heart thundered in her chest, her throat. He took a step closer until he was inside her space, dominating her space. She wanted to pull away, and yet she couldn't do so. She didn't like men who tried to dominate her—

And yet…

And yet…

Hands still tangled in her hair, he tugged her head back, exposing the column of her throat. He was so much taller than she was. She should feel vulnerable and afraid, but she did not.

"See if you *remember* this," he growled.

His head descended and her eyes dropped closed without conscious thought. He was going to kiss her, and she realized with complete shock that she wanted it. How could she want it when she didn't even like him?

But she did. And she knew she would hate herself for the weakness later.

His mouth didn't claim hers, however. Instead, she felt the touch of his lips—those hard, sensual lips—in the tender hollow of her throat. She gasped as sensation rocked her, throbbed deep in her core.

His tongue traced the indent of her collarbone. He pulled her head back farther, forcing her to arch her body against his. Her breasts thrust into his chest, into the warmth and solidity of him. Her nipples were aching peaks against the thin cups of her bikini. Surely, he knew it, too. She was embarrassed—and not embarrassed.

Her hands tangled in the silk of his shirt, clinging for dear life as his mouth moved up her throat, his kisses stinging her with need.

And then he claimed her mouth. She opened to him, let him sink into her, met him as an equal. The ache inside her chest was new, and not new. She thrust away thoughts of a possible past she couldn't remember and tried to focus on the now.

On the way he kissed her as if she was the only woman in the world. The heat between them was incredible. Had she really been chilled only moments ago? Because now she wanted to tear at the layers of clothes between them, to remove all barriers, to quench this fire the only way it could be quenched: by opening her body to him, by joining with him until the fire burned itself out.

If what he said were true, then how many times had they begun just like this? How many times had they lost themselves in each other's embrace after a scorching kiss? She couldn't ever remember being with this man—being with any man—and yet her body knew. Her body *knew*.

One hand left her hair, spanned her rib cage, his

fingers brushing beneath her breast. She couldn't stop the little moan that escaped her as he gently pinched her nipple through the fabric. The sweet spike of pleasure shot through her, connecting to her center. Liquid heat flooded her, so foreign and familiar all at once.

She became aware of something else then, as her body ached for more touching, more soft exploration. Of something thick and hard pressing into her abdomen. The first ribbon of unease rippled inside her. This couldn't be a good idea.

She couldn't give herself to him. She simply couldn't. She'd already let it go too far.

She should have never touched him. She didn't understand it, but it had been like setting a match to dry tinder.

She could feel an answering change in him, as if he too were confused and wary about what was happening between them. Before she could push him away, he stepped back, breaking the contact between their bodies.

The loss of his mouth on hers was almost a physical pain. She wanted to reach for him, pull him back, but she would not do so. She could not ever do so.

He looked completely unaffected as he bent to pick up his phone from where he'd dropped it when he'd shoved his hands into her hair.

Her lips tingled, her skin sizzled and her breathing wasn't quite the same as before he'd kissed her.

"Why did you do that?" she asked, her voice thick. It would have been so much easier if he had not.

He looked at her then, his golden skin so beautiful, his eyes still hot as they slipped over her. How many women had melted under the force of that gaze? How many had taken one look at that face and body and burned with need?

Hundreds. Thousands.

Her included.

"Because you wanted me to," he said.

She shook her head to deny it, but stopped abruptly. What would be the point? She *had* wanted him to kiss her. But she knew what it felt like now, and she would never be so weak again. "Now that you have, I'd like you to go," she said firmly.

"You and I both know that's not going to happen, Isabella."

Isabella drew in a sharp breath. The man had a hearing problem. "You can't force me to return to Jahfar. I'm an American citizen, and there are laws here that prevent such things."

He looked so coolly elegant, in spite of his casual clothing, in spite of the way she'd crushed his shirt in her fists and wrinkled the fine silk.

"Nevertheless, you will go—"

"There's no reason," she insisted.

"There is every reason!" he thundered, the fine edge of his temper bared at last. "You will cease being so selfish, Isabella. You will do this for Rafiq, if for no other reason."

Isabella hugged herself as a river of ice water poured down her spine. She was tired and confused and ready for this to be over. "I'm sorry you think I'm being selfish, but I've told you the truth. I don't know you. And I don't know who Rafiq is, either."

Adan's eyes were so cold in his handsome face. Like black ice as he gazed at her with unconcealed contempt. He was angrier than she'd yet seen him.

He pronounced the next words very precisely, each one carefully measured, each one like a blow to her subconscious as the full effect landed on her with the force of a sandstorm whipping through a purple Jahfaran sky.

"Rafiq is our son."

CHAPTER THREE

THE interior of Adan's private jet was sumptuous, but Isabella hardly noticed. She'd been in shock since the moment he'd told her they had a child. It had felt as if someone was slicing into her heart with a rusty knife. How could she have given birth to a child and not know it?

It was surreal.

But as much as her mind kept telling her that everything he said was impossible, her heart whispered doubts. Her heart said that something had happened to her two years ago, and that a car wreck didn't explain it nearly as well as she would like.

She'd gone with him then. She'd let him take her back to her condo where she'd packed a suitcase and called the landlord to tell him she would be gone for a couple of weeks. Adan had stood by impassively, not saying a word as she'd readied herself. He'd looked around the small living space as if it were completely foreign to him. As if he were horrified she would live there.

Which, she supposed, he probably was. He was a prince of Jahfar. Princes did not live in studios that weren't much bigger than a large shoebox.

They'd ridden to the airport in silence, then boarded

the sleek Boeing business jet and taken off shortly thereafter. Now they were somewhere high over the Pacific Ocean, and Isabella sat in a large reclining leather chair and stared out the window at nothing but blackness. On a small table in front of her was an untouched glass of papaya juice. She shivered involuntarily. She'd put on a pair of jeans and a T-shirt and grabbed a light jacket, but still she was cold.

"Would you like a blanket, ma'am?" one of the flight attendants asked.

"Thank you, yes," Isabella replied. Her voice sounded scratchy, distant, as if she weren't accustomed to using it. The attendant returned with the blanket and a pillow. Isabella wrapped herself in the plush fabric. This wasn't one of those cheap excuses for a blanket used on major airlines these days. It was thick and soft and smelled like spice.

A few moments later, Adan sank into the chair across from her. She hadn't seen him since shortly after they'd gotten airborne. He'd said he had business to attend to and had disappeared into his private office. Now, he clutched a sheaf of papers. His gaze was disturbing. She wasn't sure if it was because of the kiss they'd shared in Ka Nui's, or simply because he caused something to tighten inside her every time he looked at her.

Or maybe it was because he despised her.

"You haven't touched your drink," he said.

"I'm not thirsty." She dropped her gaze, conscious suddenly that she was still wearing heavy stage makeup. She hadn't thought to wash her face in the rush to grab her suitcase and change clothes. He hadn't rushed her, but she'd felt as if she had to hurry. As if the answers were thousands of miles away and she needed to get there as soon as possible.

"I thought you might like to see these," he said, holding out the papers.

She took them cautiously, not really certain she did want to see them, but knowing she had no choice but to look. For herself. For her sanity. Not because he was forcing her to, but because she needed to know.

Her heart began to thrum.

She looked at the first sheet. It was an article from *Al-Arab Jahfar*.

Prince Weds Daughter of Prominent Businessman.

There was a photo of her and Adan. He was so handsome in his traditional clothing, with a ceremonial dagger at his waist. He looked solemn, as if he were performing a duty.

Which he no doubt had been. *We met a week before the wedding...*

She was smiling, but she didn't look happy. Her dress was a beaded silk *abaya* in a deep saffron color. She wore the sheerest *hijab*, the fabric filmy and beautiful where it skimmed her hair.

She glanced up, saw Adan watching her closely. He was sprawled in his chair like a potentate, one elbow propped on the armrest, his index finger sliding absently back and forth over his bottom lip. His dark eyes gave nothing away.

Isabella slid the article to the bottom of the pile. The next one sent her heart into her throat.

It was a birth announcement. Rafiq ibn Adan Al Dhakir, born April fourth.

Tears pressed against the backs of her eyes. She wanted to sob. She bit her lip, hard, to stop the tears from coming. She wanted to shove the papers at him and tell him to take them away, but gritted her teeth and told herself she would do this. She would look at them and she would survive it.

Because everything she'd known, everything she'd believed—about herself, about her parents—was shattered and lying broken at her feet. She wasn't who she thought she was.

She was this woman, this Princess Isabella Al Dhakir, who had a baby and a husband. Who should have had a perfect life, but who was sitting here broken and alone.

She uncovered the next article with trembling fingers.

This one proclaimed her missing. From her father's house, where she'd gone to visit after the birth of her child. Evidence suggested she'd walked into the desert. A sandstorm had stopped the rescue effort for three days. When it resumed, there was no trace of her.

She thought of her father's house at the edge of the wilds of Jahfar. He loved to tame nature. He had a pool, fountains and grass on the edge of the hottest, starkest land imaginable.

And she had willingly walked alone into that desert?

The fourth article made the numbness creep over her again. It was small, a quarter sheet, the words stark against the white background.

Dead...

She quickly flipped to the next page. A marriage

contract, spelling out everything her father and Adan had agreed to. She didn't read it. She didn't need to.

She closed her eyes and dropped the papers on the table between them, then clasped her hands in her lap so he wouldn't see them shaking. She was his wife. The mother of his child.

And she couldn't remember any of it. Isabella tried so hard to conjure up an image of a baby in her arms, but she couldn't do it.

What was wrong with her? How could a mother forget her own baby? She turned her head away on the seat back and dug her fingernails into her palms. She would not cry. She could not cry in front of him. She couldn't be weak.

"Do you still wish to deny the truth?" Adan asked.

She shook her head, unable to speak for fear she would lose control.

"Why did you do it, Isabella? Why did you leave your baby son? Did you not think of him even once?"

It took her several moments to answer.

"I don't remember doing it," she forced out, her voice barely more than a whisper. "I don't remember anything about that…that night. In the newspaper."

She thought he wouldn't believe her, that he would demand to know the truth, demand she stop lying. But he blew out a breath and looked away before turning to pierce her with his dark stare again. "Tell me what you do know, then. Tell me how you got to Hawaii."

She wanted to be defiant, but she was too mentally drained to conjure up even a hint of strength. "I was in Jahfar, and then I was at my mother's house in South Carolina," she said, hugging the blanket tighter. "I don't remember when I left, or how I got there. My father says it's because of the accident. Because I hit my head in the crash and was in a coma for five weeks. I don't remember the accident, but the doctor said that was normal.

"After, I spent time recuperating at my mother's before I moved out on my own."

"You didn't want to return to Jahfar?"

"No, not really. I thought of it from time to time, but my father told me to stay in the States. He said he traveled a lot now, and there was no reason for me to return yet."

"Hawaii is rather far from South Carolina," he mused.

It was, and yet she'd been pulled there by homesickness. "I missed the sea, and the palms. I went there for a short vacation but ended up staying."

"Why did you change your name?"

"I didn't change it. Bella Tyler is a stage name," she said, not wanting to admit that she'd wanted to be someone else, that calling herself by another name had been an effort to make her feel different. More confident. Less alone.

"And why were you singing in a club, Isabella? Did you need money?"

He no doubt thought so based on the size of her condo, but it was perfectly adequate for Maui. And more expensive than he might imagine.

"No. My father sent me plenty. But I sang karaoke one day, for fun. The next I knew, I was performing."

A disapproving frown made his sensual mouth seem hard. "A lounge singer."

Isabella felt heat prickle over her skin. "I *like* to sing.

I've always liked to sing. And I'm good at it," she said proudly.

"I never heard you sing before tonight."

"I sang plenty growing up, but it was for myself. If I never sang for you, then I suppose I was afraid to. Afraid you would disapprove."

"I might not have," he said softly.

"I must have thought so."

"Perhaps you did." He was unapologetic.

Isabella clutched the blanket in a fist. This was such an odd conversation. She was married to this man, and yet he was a stranger to her. They were strangers to each other, if this conversation was anything to go by.

"We must not have spent a lot of time together," she ventured.

"Enough," he said, his eyes suddenly hot, intense.

Isabella dipped her head, hoping she wasn't blushing. Clearly she wasn't a virgin, and yet she couldn't remember anything about her first sexual experience with him. About *any* sexual experience with him.

"How long were we married before…the baby?"

"You were pregnant the first month. And you disappeared only a month after Rafiq was born."

She pressed a hand to her stomach beneath the blanket. It was so hard to imagine she'd ever been pregnant. "So we weren't together a year."

He gave his head a shake. "Not quite, no."

She was trying so hard to process it. Because they *were* married. He hadn't faked a bunch of documents to prove it to her. These were printed copies of actual newspaper articles.

Far more likely—and harder to understand, quite honestly—was the fact her parents had lied. Oh, she didn't really expect that her mother had orchestrated this fiction Isabella had been living with—or that she'd had a problem going along with it. No, it was her father who'd done so.

And Isabella couldn't figure out why.

Was Adan abusive? Had her hurt her? Was her father simply being protective?

She considered it, but she didn't believe that was the case. Because Adan had been very angry with her, yes, and he'd been arrogant and presumptuous. But he hadn't for one moment made her feel physically threatened. If he had, she wouldn't be here.

Or at least not willingly.

She was uncomfortable with him—but not because she feared him.

Isabella pressed two fingers to her temple. It was so much to process.

"Does your head hurt?" Adan asked suddenly.

She was surprised at the answer. "Yes." She'd been so focused that she hadn't realized her temple was beginning to throb. Soon, the headache would spread to the other side. And she'd left her migraine medicine on the kitchen counter. She didn't get them often, but when she did, they weren't in the least bit pleasant.

Adan pressed a button on his seat and a flight attendant appeared. He ordered a glass of water and some ibuprofen. When it arrived, she gulped down the tablets, though she didn't expect they would do any good.

"Perhaps you should sleep," he said. "There's a bedroom at the back, and a bathroom where you can wash your face."

She should sleep, and yet she couldn't quite yet. "Do you have a picture of him?" she asked quietly.

The corners of his mouth grew tight. Then he pulled out his cell phone and pressed a few buttons. When he held it out to her, the breath caught in her throat.

The little boy staring at the camera was adorable, of course. But it was more than that. She gazed at his face in wonder, searching for signs of her own features. She saw Adan easily in the dark hair and dark eyes. But the chin, that was hers. And the shape of the nose.

A tear slipped free and slid down her cheek. "He's two now?"

Adan nodded as he took the phone back. She wasn't ready to stop looking at the photo, and yet she couldn't ask him to let her see it again.

She'd missed so much. So damn much. His first word. His first step. She scrubbed a hand across her face. Her head throbbed. Her stomach churned. She wasn't sure if it was the headache or the heartache causing it, but she felt physically ill.

Isabella shot to her feet. Adan rose with the grace of a hunting panther, his brows drawn together. "What is wrong?"

"I have to—the bathroom."

Adan pointed and Isabella bolted for the door. She made it just in time, heaving the contents of her stomach into the toilet. When she finally straightened, she caught sight of her face in the mirror. She looked like hell. Like a girl who'd got into her mother's makeup and put way too much on in an effort to look more grown-up.

Isabella turned on the taps—bronze taps on an airplane, so much fancier than the usual airline bathroom—and began to scrub her face with hot water and soap. The tears started to flow as she scrubbed. She tried to stop it at first, but then decided to let herself cry. He would never hear her with the water running.

She scrubbed hard, as if she could scrub away the past two years and clean her memory free of the black curtain cloaking it at the same time. Her head continued to pound, but she cried and scrubbed until the makeup was gone and her tears were finished.

She hoped Adan would be gone by the time she returned to her seat—in his office, or sleeping in one of the staterooms—but she wasn't that lucky.

He looked up as she approached. His expression didn't change, but she was certain he hadn't missed a thing. She looked like hell. Her face was pink and her eyes, though not puffy yet, soon would be from the crying.

"You are ill?" he asked.

"It's the migraine," she replied, shrugging. "If I have my medicine, it doesn't get that bad, but without it…"

"You did not bring this medicine, I take it."

"I was a bit preoccupied."

"Tell me the name of this drug," he commanded. "It will be waiting for you when we arrive in Jahfar."

She said the name, then folded herself back into the reclining chair.

"You should lie down on a bed."

She waved a hand. "I'd rather not walk that far right now, if you don't mind."

He rose, and before she knew what he was about to do, he'd come around to her chair and reached for her. She started to protest, but her head hurt too badly to put up much of a fight as she was lifted against his chest.

He was warm, hard and so solid. She felt safe for the first time in years. *Safe.*

And yet it was an illusion. Now, more than ever, she needed to guard herself against emotion. Because she was emotionally raw right now, vulnerable.

She felt so much. *Too much.*

She could feel his heart beating strong beneath the palm she'd rested on his chest, could smell the delicious spicy male scent of him. He carried her toward the back of the plane and into a room that contained a double-size bed. The sheets were folded down already, and the lights were dim. Heaven for her throbbing head.

He set her on the bed and she lay back, uncaring that she wore jeans. Adan slipped her shoes from her feet and then pulled the blanket over her. She closed her eyes, unable to watch him as he cared for her.

Because he didn't *really* care for her, did he?

"Sleep, Isabella," he said.

"Adan," she said when he was at the door.

"Yes?"

She swallowed. Her throat hurt from crying. "I'm sorry."

He merely inclined his head before pulling the door shut with a sharp click.

Adan didn't sleep well. He kept tossing and turning, kicking off the covers, pulling them back again. In the next cabin, he imagined Isabella huddled beneath the blankets and sleeping soundly.

He had to admit, when she'd walked out of the bathroom earlier with her face scrubbed clean, he'd been gutted by her expression. She'd been crying, he could tell that right away. Her skin had been pink from the hot water she must have used, but her nose was redder and her eyes were bloodshot. She looked as though she'd been through hell.

And maybe she had. She'd seemed so stunned as she'd absorbed the news about their marriage, about Rafiq. About her *death*.

Adan pressed his closed fist to his forehead. He had no room for sympathy for her. He had to do what he'd come here to do. His country depended on it. His son depended on it.

He would not risk Rafiq's happiness. Isabella was his mother, but what kind of mother was she? She'd abandoned her baby. Even if she truly didn't remember doing it, she had. And she'd been in possession of all her faculties at the time. What had happened after, he did not know, but she'd chosen to leave.

Whether she'd truly walked into the desert or whether it was a fiction she'd cooked up to cover her tracks, he wasn't certain. But whatever the truth, her father had helped her.

He would deal with Hassan Maro soon enough.

Right now, he had to deal with Isabella.

Adan threw back the covers. There was no sense in lying here any longer when he could get some work done instead. After he'd showered and shaved, he dressed in a white *dishdasha* and the traditional dark red *keffiyeh* of Jahfar.

A new shift of flight attendants was busily preparing breakfast in the galley. When they saw him, all activity immediately stopped as they dipped into deep curtsies and bows. He was still getting used to it, really. As a prince, he'd received obeisance, but not to the level he now did as a king. It was disconcerting sometimes. He was impatient, wanted to cut right to the matter, but he realized—thanks to Mahmoud's tutelage—that the forms were still important to people. It set him apart, and there were still those in Jahfar who very much appreciated the traditions of their ancient nation.

"Would you like coffee, Your Excellency?" a young man asked.

"Yes, thank you," Adan replied. "Bring it to my office."

He went into the large space and sat down behind the big wooden desk. His computer fired up instantly, and he checked email. Then he brought up a window and typed in a search phrase: *selective amnesia.*

The coffee arrived, and Adan drank it while he read about dissociative amnesia, systematized amnesia and a host of other disorders. It was possible, though rare, for someone to forget a specific person and all the events surrounding that person. Did Isabella know it, too? Had she looked it up and decided to use it as an excuse?

And yet that would have required that she had known he was coming. Adan frowned. Whatever the case, he would have her examined by a doctor when they arrived.

He picked up the phone and called his assistant in Jahfar. Adan ordered the man to request that Hassan Maro come to the palace the next day, and then asked him to find a specialist in psychological issues.

An email from Jasmine popped into his inbox as he was finishing the call. He opened it and read her chatty missive about the fitting for her bridal costume and the preparations for their wedding feast.

A shaft of guilt speared him. He hadn't told her where he was going when he'd left.

He'd known Jasmine since they were children. There'd

never been a spark between them, but they liked each other. And she was kind, gentle and would make a good mother to Rafiq, as well as to their future children.

Jasmine was a *safe* choice. The right choice.

Adan worked a while longer, eating breakfast at his desk, and then emerged to find Isabella sitting in the same seat as last night, her bare legs stretched out and crossed at the ankles as she studied the papers in her fists. The papers from last night, he realized.

She looked up as he approached. There was no smile to greet him, as there once had been. She still seemed nothing like the girl he'd married. That woman had been meek, biddable and sweetly innocent. It hit him suddenly that she'd been as forgettable as a table or a chair, or any other item you counted on but didn't notice on a daily basis.

This woman was sensual, mysterious and anything but biddable. There was a fire in her. A fire he'd never observed before. And he couldn't stop thinking about it.

Her face without all the makeup was as pure as an angel's. Her hair was as wild as yesterday, dark gold with lighter streaks that didn't come from a salon. He'd only ever seen her with long, straight locks that she usually wore in a loose chignon. This was a completely bohemian, surfer-girl style that he wasn't accustomed to.

She was wearing a dress today, a blue cotton sundress that showed too much skin for his liking, and a pair of sandals.

"You slept well?" he asked.

Her green eyes were still smoky, though not as smoky as yesterday when they'd been surrounded in dark makeup. She looked troubled, not rested.

"As well as can be expected, I guess."

He understood the sentiment.

"We will arrive in Jahfar in another three hours or so," he said.

She set the papers aside. "And what happens then, Adan?"

"Many things, I imagine," he replied, purposely keeping it vague.

"When can I see…Rafiq?"

He noticed that she swallowed before she said his son's name. *His* son, not hers. Not anymore. She'd given up that right two years ago. And he would not subject Rafiq to any confusion, not when he was about to marry Jasmine.

"You cannot, I'm afraid. It is out of the question."

CHAPTER FOUR

ISABELLA stared up at him, wondering if the shock and hurt she felt were showing on her face, or if it was only inside that she was being clawed to ribbons. The pain was immense, but she refused to cry. She was finished with crying. She'd cried in the bathroom and she'd cried in her bed in the night while the plane's engines droned endlessly on, but she would not cry again.

Nor would she accept his decrees as if he were her own personal dictator.

"Perhaps I shouldn't have phrased it that way," she said. "It wasn't truly a question."

He looked so hard and handsome in his *dishdasha* and headdress. His dark eyes glittered in that hawklike face. His lips, no matter how they flattened or frowned or grew firm with irritation, managed to be much more sexy than she would like them to be.

"You cannot see him," he pronounced. "It will confuse him."

Anger burst in her belly like a firecracker. "He's two, Adan. How will it confuse him?"

He blew out a hard breath. "You know nothing of him. You will not presume to tell me what is best for *my* son."

"Our son."

He got to his feet in a swirl of robes. Out of the corner of her eye, she saw one of the flight attendants backing away. Everyone treated him as if he were a god. As if he controlled their destinies and made the sun shine or the rain fall on their rooftops.

She would not do the same.

Isabella shot to her feet and faced him squarely. Everything she'd known about herself and her life was in the gutter now, and he thought she would meekly accept his decrees? Especially a decree that regarded her child?

"I'm his mother," she said before he could turn and walk away from her.

"You gave birth to him," Adan snapped. "But it takes more than that to make a mother."

She clenched her hands into fists at her side. Her heart pounded, and the remnants of her headache made her temples throb oh so lightly.

"I realize that."

"Do you?" he said, his jaw rigid with anger. "When, precisely, did you have this revelation?"

"Adan—"

"Did you consider it in the moments before you made your decision? Those last moments before you left your infant alone in your father's house?"

Every word was like a physical blow. And yet she could not back down. She had to be firm, had to stand up under the onslaught, or be crushed forever by his fury and derision.

"I left him alone? There was no one else in the house?"

His jaw flexed. "There were servants, but that's not the same as a mother."

Her heart hurt. Why had she done such a thing? *Why?* "And you would continue to deprive him of a mother now that you've found me?"

"He does not need you," Adan said, and her heart shattered anew.

"How do you know?" she flung at him. "Is this merely because you've decreed it must be? Or do you truly know what's in the mind of a child?"

"Don't test my patience, Isabella." His voice was a feral growl.

And she didn't care. She took a step closer, hands on hips, and glared up into his glittering obsidian eyes. "Then why in the hell am I here, Adan? What do you want from me?"

"You know what I want. You've already named it."

Her blood began to beat harder in her veins. Her head felt light suddenly. Dark spots swam in her vision.

No. She would not be so silly as to pass out simply because he wanted a divorce.

She didn't really know him. Didn't love him. His rejection shouldn't matter.

It *didn't* matter.

But the child did. Rafiq. Her baby. The baby who was also a stranger to her, but who was a part of her flesh and blood. He carried her DNA. He was half her. She would not give him up when she'd just found him.

"I won't divorce you," she said, her voice as low and hard as she could make it. It didn't even come close to his, however.

"You don't have a choice, Isabella. Have you forgotten that we are Jahfaran?"

She thrust her chin out and shoved her hair from her face. "By Jahfaran you mean that you hold all the power. No, I haven't forgotten that. But I don't intend to make it easy for you."

He blinked. "You," he said very dangerously, "don't intend to make it easy for me?"

And then he burst into laughter, startling her with the richness of the sound. It was funny, of course, because he was right: she had no power. There was nothing she could do, really.

Still, she didn't intend to go down easily. "I'll fight you. Whatever it takes, I'll do it. I won't let you take my child away from me before I've ever had the chance to know him."

He closed the distance between them, looming over her like a tall and menacing shadow. "You made your choice two years ago. You have nothing to fight me with."

They stared at each other for several moments.

And then he lifted his hand. She flinched, but refused to cower. His fingers touched her—so softly, so lightly. They stroked down her cheek, her neck, back up the other side to the opposite cheek. Rivulets of flame trailed in their wake. Her skin prickled with heat, cooled and then heated again.

Her lips parted, her tongue darting out to moisten them. His gaze sharpened, followed the motion.

"You had it all, Isabella," he said softly, so very softly. "A wealthy husband, a child and the possibility of more. But it wasn't enough for you. *We* weren't enough for you. Tell me why I would ever give you that chance again."

She swallowed. His eyes were full of emotion, though she wasn't sure which emotion.

A thought struck her like a lightning bolt. She could hardly believe it was possible, considering how he'd told her they'd barely known one another, but what if it was? What if it explained everything?

"Were you..." She swallowed again. "Were you in love with me? Is that why you're so angry?"

He looked surprised. But then he shook his head slowly, his eyes mocking her. "Not at all. It was you who loved me."

She stiffened beneath his touch, that soft stroking of her skin that she shouldn't be allowing and yet couldn't seem to pull away from. "How do you know that?"

This time the expression on his face was one of pity. "Because you told me so."

"I don't believe you," she said automatically. If she'd been in love with this man, wouldn't she have known it? Wouldn't she feel some sort of connection even now, even with her memory damaged?

"Believe what you wish, Isabella. It does not change the truth." His hand dropped away. She wanted to protest, wanted to ask him to keep touching her, but she did not. "And yet it was a lie, wasn't it? Because if you had loved me—loved us—you would not have run away."

"This is very convenient for you," she said, her soul aching. "If I protest or disagree, you simply tell me that I did this terrible thing, knowing I cannot argue with you. Knowing that I don't remember what truly happened." She put her fists on her hips and glared at him. "How do I know you weren't involved? What if everything *you* say is a lie?"

"There was a time long ago in Jahfar," he said, "when calling me a liar would have got you a death sentence."

"Well, thank God we live in enlightened times!" she snorted.

Behind Adan, another flight attendant had stopped with one foot in the air as if she had been arrested in motion. She pivoted and started to walk away.

"Oh, for God's sake," Isabella exploded. "Why does everyone tiptoe around you like you're about to chop off their heads?"

She hurried past Adan and caught up with the woman. "If you wish to speak to him, please come do so."

The girl bowed her head. "His Excellency is busy. I will come another time."

Isabella's blood boiled. She'd had it with his high-handedness, and she didn't care if he was the prince of the universe. People had jobs to do, and they couldn't do it with him carrying on like a wounded lion.

"You wished to ask if we wanted drinks? Food?"

"Drinks, Your Highness."

Isabella was taken aback at the title and almost corrected the girl.

Until she remembered. She *was* a princess, at least for the moment, and though the staff hadn't seemed to know it when she'd boarded, they certainly knew so now that she and Adan had been arguing so loudly.

"I would like water with lemon, please." She turned to look at Adan, who was still glowering in the same spot. "Your Worship, would you like anything to drink?"

She thought she saw his jaw grinding. "No."

"Very well." She turned back to the girl. "I'll just have that water, then."

"Yes, Your Highness." She dipped into a curtsey and was gone, hurrying toward the galley at double speed.

"I don't know how you live with yourself," Isabella

said. "Terrorizing women, demanding obedience and glaring at everything in sight. Wouldn't you like, just once, for someone to *want* to talk to you without being terrified about what you'll do or say?"

His expression was stone. "This will no doubt come as a surprise to you, but I don't terrorize anyone. They obey me because it is my due."

Isabella returned to her seat and sank down into it. "You are a deluded man, then. Because from where I'm sitting, you pretty much terrorize everyone."

"You don't seem terrorized," he remarked somewhat wryly.

"I'm trying very hard not to be."

The flight attendant returned with a glass of mineral water and a plate of sliced lemons. She set it on the table in front of Isabella and curtsied again. "Will that be all, Your Highness?"

"Thank you, yes."

The girl then asked Adan if he would like anything after all. He replied that he would not, and she disappeared into the galley.

Isabella squeezed a lemon slice into the glass and sipped the cool, bubbly water. It felt good against her throat, which was sore from a night of singing and crying. She pointedly ignored Adan, staring out the window instead. It was day now, and they were high over the clouds.

"You have changed, Isabella."

She looked up at him, her heart flipping at the heat and anger in those dark, dark eyes. "Everything has changed," she said softly. "It's adapt or die. I prefer to adapt."

"You will soon be returning to Hawaii, so do not adapt too much."

Her stomach tightened, but she refused to react. "You won't frighten me away, Adan. No matter what you do, you won't frighten me away."

"It would be unwise of you to plan for a future in Jahfar," he warned. "You will only be there as long as it takes to sort out the legal tangle of you being alive rather than dead."

"I will *not* be silent. And I will not fade away into the night like a ghost, no matter how you might wish it."

He considered her for a long moment. "And yet, that is not your choice to make."

Stepping off the plane onto Jahfaran soil was like stepping from a refrigerator into a blast furnace. The sun beat down on the white tarmac, reflecting light into her eyes. Isabella wore sunglasses, but she felt as if her corneas were burning nonetheless.

She'd forgotten how bright, how hot, how desolate Jahfar could be. Especially compared to the lush verdancy of Hawaii.

In the distance, date palms lined the runway. Farther away, stark sandstone mountains loomed in the background. It was home, and it was foreign.

Three black Mercedes limousines sat nearby, and a team of dark-suited men with earpieces waited stoically beside them. Several men in white *dishdashas,* wearing traditional *keffiyehs,* stood in a cluster near the bottom of the stairs. A red carpet had been rolled out from the plane to the cars.

Adan preceded her down the stairs. The men at the bottom sank to their knees and touched their heads to the ground as he approached. Isabella stopped short. This was the greeting given to the ruler, not to a royal family member.

Adan spoke with the men, and then they were standing and he was striding down the carpet toward the cars. She was stuck in place, trying to process what she'd just seen, and wanting more than anything to turn around and climb back up the stairs. Part of her—the small, scared part—wanted to rewind the past twenty-four hours and go back to the way it was before she'd known about Adan and their son.

Adan reached the car and turned to look at her. At that moment, something inside her broke loose, broke her foothold on the steps, and she was running down them and hurrying to his side. She would not let him leave her behind. She would not cower from this, or from the hard truths that awaited her when she spoke with her father again.

He stepped back to let her inside the car, then climbed in beside her. The door shut solidly behind them and then the car was moving.

Isabella ran a nervous hand along the skirt of her sundress. Where was her bravery of earlier? Where was the woman who'd stood toe-to-toe with him? Who had challenged him and threatened him?

She didn't know, but she did know she was having trouble catching her breath. Moisture pooled in the valley between her breasts. She should not have run in this heat. She'd been gone too long and she was no longer accustomed to it.

Adan reached down into what she realized was a small refrigerator and then thrust a bottle of cold water at her. "Drink this before you pass out."

Isabella twisted the top off and took a gulp. "I'd forgotten how hot Jahfar is," she said, hoping her voice didn't betray her unease. She wanted to appear calm, unruffled, though she was anything but.

"You seem to have trouble remembering quite a lot of things," Adan said coolly.

Isabella ignored the taunt. "That was the greeting for a king."

She couldn't see his eyes behind his mirrored sunglasses. But his lips thinned. "Precisely."

"You are the king? I thought the king was an Al Nasri." Her heart was beginning to throb. What had she walked into? What awful, tangled mess was this?

"My cousin and his family died in a boating accident last year. I became my uncle's heir, as I am the oldest of my brothers. My uncle died a little over a week ago."

Her breath stopped in her chest. It was too much. "I am not… I can't be…"

"The queen? No, you aren't," he said firmly. "Nor will you be."

"But if you are king?"

His mouth turned down. "I cannot be formally invested until I am married. It is the law. I am the acting king until the coronation."

Isabella resisted the urge to roll the cold bottle against her neck and chest. She would never be cool enough, especially now that her heart beat so hard and her skin prickled with the nearness of this man. "I'm afraid I don't understand. You *are* married."

He slipped the glasses from his face and tossed them down on the seat beside him. His eyes speared her, so hard and cold in the frame of his handsome face. And hot. How did they manage to be hot, as well?

"Twenty-four hours ago I was a widower. You have thrown a bit of a spanner in the works, as the charming saying goes—but we will take care of that shortly. Once we do, I can proceed with the wedding that you have interrupted."

"Wedding? You're getting married?"

"This is what I have said."

Hurt and fury warred within her. Of course he would have moved on, and of course he would have had to remarry if he thought she were dead. But now that she was back? Now that she knew they had a child together?

"Are you in love with her?" she asked. Because if he was, if he'd found someone he adored who adored him in return, how could she stand between them?

And how could she *not,* when her child's future was at stake?

"That is none of your concern," he said shortly.

Her heart thrummed. "That means no, then. Because if you were, you wouldn't mind saying it."

His fingers drummed the leather seat. "You do not know this."

"I do," she insisted. "No one in love minds that question. Unless the relationship is forbidden for some reason."

His gaze sharpened. "Have you been in love recently, Isabella? Do you speak from experience?"

She dropped her gaze, unwilling to let him see even an ounce of her loneliness over the past couple of years. Her certainty that someone was out there for her, but that she had not yet found him.

"No."

He gripped her chin in his fingers and forced her head

up. His eyes searched hers. "You belong to me, *habibti*. I would not take it kindly if you have a lover."

"I don't see why it would matter," she said. "You can't wait to be rid of me."

Something flashed across his face—and then he abruptly let her go. "Yes, this is true. The sooner it is done, the better. It is time Rafiq had a proper mother."

It was as if he'd taken a hot dagger and thrust it through her heart. Isabella had to restrain herself from doing violence to him. He was insensitive, brutal, cold.

No doubt she'd be thrown into the depths of Port Jahfar's dankest prison, should she raise a hand to their king, and yet that wasn't what stopped her. It was the thought of her baby.

"You are the vilest person I know, do you realize that? Why did you bring me here? Why did you ever come find me if all you wanted to do was shatter my heart like this? You lied when you said I was in love with you. I could never, *ever* have loved a man like you."

"That's a very charming speech," he said. "But you know why you're here. If I had not come for you, I would be committing a terrible fraud when I take a new wife and queen."

"Of course," she said bitterly. "It's all about *you*. About your feelings and your wants. You could care less about mine. And you damn sure could care less about our little boy's!"

"Be careful what you say to me, Isabella," he growled. "Jahfar is not so modern as you might wish, and if you continue to push me, you will find out precisely how ruthless I can be."

"I think I already know," she flung at him.

"You really don't," he said silkily.

"What could be more ruthless than separating a mother and child?"

His eyes narrowed, the corners crinkling with years of sun and wind. She could see the harshness of the desert in his face, the struggle for survival that punctuated life in that wilderness. He was a king, but he wasn't tame by any standard—would never be tame.

She shivered, as if in premonition.

His words were coated in ice. "Abandoning a child to grow up without a mother is far more ruthless than anything I have ever done."

CHAPTER FIVE

ADAN sat at the large carved desk in his office and stared stonily at his private solicitor. "What do you mean, my divorce will take *some* time?"

The solicitor cleared his throat. "The marriage contract with Isabella Maro is very clear, Your Excellency. If she does not agree to the divorce, then only if she is barren can you set aside the contract. This is not an issue, clearly."

Adan's blood pressure skyrocketed.

"But there are extenuating circumstances," the man continued, "and those will be a factor in presenting our case that your marriage should be dissolved, with or without her agreement."

Adan tossed his pen down on the desk with a sharp crack. Damn her! She was proving to be nothing but trouble after all. He'd read the contract before he'd ever signed it, but, of course, nothing about it had been out of the ordinary. Though it was true that Jahfaran men had much of the power, women were not without protection. He could not divorce her for no reason.

He shoved to his feet and paced over to the window. "What about the coronation?"

The solicitor cleared his throat. "You are married and

can proceed. But no crowned king of Jahfar has ever divorced his queen."

Adan turned to look at the man. "But *can* it be done?"

He was determined that Isabella was not going to win this battle by default. She was not the sort of woman he wanted to mother his son. Rafiq's welfare was paramount. There was nothing more important to him.

"I am not certain of it, Your Excellency. There is no precedent to go by."

"Keep me informed," Adan said by way of dismissal. The solicitor bowed and Mahmoud showed him out.

Adan's gut burned with rage at the predicament he now found himself in. But there was something more swirling inside him, some other feeling that had an edge of…anticipation?

He shoved the thought aside. What was there to anticipate? Isabella infuriated him and the longer he spent in her company, the more he wanted to grasp her by the shoulders and…

Kiss her.

No. He wanted to shake her, not kiss her.

But you do want to kiss her. Everywhere.

No, he thought. *No.*

He'd kissed her once, and that had been enough. She was poisonous; he would not risk bringing her into Rafiq's life again. He did not know why she'd left them, but it was undeniable that she had done so. Just as it was undeniable that she now felt guilty for it.

Was guilt the only reason she wanted to see Rafiq, the only reason she claimed to want to be a part of his life? And what would happen when she realized that little boys were energetic and messy, that they needed love and discipline and parents who put their welfare first?

He would not take that chance. He knew what it was like to have a mother whose love you craved, but who would rather see you when you were cleaned and groomed and dressed like a perfect little boy so she could show you off to her friends.

Her friends would *ooh* and *aah* and pinch your cheeks.

And then you would be sent back to the nursery with your nanny, the woman who would clean your scrapes, wipe your tears and mitigate your fights with your brothers on a daily basis. The woman who really loved you and raised you as if you were her child, because your own mother claimed that children were too much for her delicate nerves.

He did not want that for his son. He wanted a woman who loved Rafiq with her whole heart, and who would never see him as an inconvenience or a burden. Jasmine was that woman, not Isabella.

Not only that, but he was also determined not to be forced into spending the rest of his life with a woman he didn't trust. A woman he despised.

A woman he wanted so badly he could taste it.

Adan swore under his breath. How could he want her? How could he feel this pull of attraction for her, but not for Jasmine? How could he want to strip that damn blue dress off her body and find her sweet feminine center with his fingers and tongue before plunging deeply into her body in order to slake this craving?

He had never been ruled by desire. Had never allowed his need for a woman to override his good sense. He remembered delighting in Isabella's body before, but they'd been newly wed and it was his duty to get her with child.

Liar.

It had been more than that, and he knew it. He'd wanted her then, and he wanted her now. In spite of her lack of personality back then, in spite of her unsuitability now.

He would not act on the compulsion, however, no matter how long the divorce took. There was nothing good that could come of it. He'd been weak when he'd kissed her in Hawaii, but he would not be so weak again.

For Rafiq's sake, he would not be weak.

Isabella didn't remember ever having been to the palace before, though for all she knew, she had been. The whitewashed sandstone was inlaid with gold and por-celain tiles until the whole structure seemed to gleam in the sunshine. But that hadn't been the most amazing thing.

The most amazing thing about the palace was the approach. The marble fountains and statuary, the palms, the lush tropical plants and the acres of green grass that were indicative of fabulous wealth in such a hot and water-conscious country. Port Jahfar sat on the Arabian Sea, but the water had to be desalinated before it could be used to care for plants. And it took massive amounts of water to make grass grow in Jahfar.

After their arrival, she'd been shown to a suite of rooms and left on her own for the past several hours, with the exception of a visit from a doctor who wanted to ask questions about her memory. She'd answered as truthfully as she could. He hadn't been able to enlighten her about her condition in any way, but he'd seemed satisfied by her answers.

She'd tried to leave her room afterward, but a servant had been assigned to her whose single duty, it seemed, was to keep her from doing so.

Finally, after exploring her quarters, she'd taken up residence in a window seat that afforded her a view of the sea beyond the palace's gardens. She was full of restless energy, and frustrated that she had no way to use it. There was no computer, no books, no television, nothing to occupy her time. There was a desk and some writing paper, and there were several seating areas with comfortable furniture, but nothing else of note.

Out of boredom, she decided to sing. First, she sang an old Jahfaran song that her father had taught her. Then she moved into the songs she'd sang at Ka Nui's. She ran through several of them, letting the songs reach deep into her and pull out the sadness and heartbreak.

This was the first time she'd sung with the knowledge that she was a mother and wife, and the hollowness that had always been there while she sang now made sense. She understood where that core of loneliness was coming from now, and she ached with the knowledge of what she'd lost.

She wanted her child. She wanted to see him and hold him. She didn't know what it felt like to be a mother, but she could think of nothing else now that she knew she'd had a baby. Always before, she'd been somewhat wary of children. She didn't know what to say to them, didn't know how to soothe them or amuse them.

But now, in the space of a few hours, she was surprised at how desperately she wanted to hold a child.

Her child. She wouldn't know what to say or do, but she would learn.

She *wanted* to learn.

And Adan wanted to deprive her of that. Anger welled up inside her, and desperation. How could she fight a king? She was here so he could divorce her, no other reason. He would hustle her out of the palace and back to Hawaii as soon as it was done. Tonight, perhaps.

She stood up and paced to the door in frustration. She knew she'd find a servant sitting on the other side, but what if he was gone? It might be her one and only chance to escape this room. Isabella jerked open the door—and froze, the song in her throat dying away.

The servant was indeed sitting beside the door, but it was the old woman standing in the corridor, holding a small child, that had Isabella's full attention.

The boy's eyes were fixed on her, his little mouth hanging open in surprise. Her eyes drank him in greedily. He had the black curls and eyes of his father—but he had her nose and chin. He was the most beautiful little boy she'd ever seen.

She wanted to reach for him, but he suddenly burst into tears.

"Oh, no, please, I'm sorry," she said, taking a step toward them with her hand held out. But then she stopped, her heart breaking as Rafiq continued to cry. She desperately wanted to hold him and soothe him, but he didn't know her. He turned his head into the neck of the old woman and wailed.

"It's not your fault, *sitt,*" she said. "He wants you to sing. We stopped because of the singing."

Isabella bit back a choked sound that was half sob,

half laugh. Her heart ached, and yet it was swelling with love for this baby who was half hers.

"Of course," she said. "But why don't you come in, it will be more comfortable. And then I will sing for as long as he likes."

The woman's eyes narrowed, as if she were seeing Isabella for the first time. She ran her hand up and down the boy's back, crooning to him. Then she glanced down at the child in her arms and back at Isabella, as if she were considering something.

"Yes," she said after a long pause. "We will come."

Adan shoved back from his desk. It was time to call it a day. After the solicitor had left, he'd spoken with Jasmine and told her the truth of what was going on. She'd been so silent on the other end of the phone. And then she'd said, "Perhaps it is for the best."

"It is not what I want," he'd replied. "She is not what I want."

Jasmine's warm voice poured through the line like sweet honey. "She is still your wife, and the mother of your child. I think she has been brought back to you for a reason."

They'd spoken some more, about the wedding, about the necessity of putting any plans on hold and about the coronation. Jasmine was understanding, gracious, and he grew angrier and angrier as he talked to her. Not with her, but with the woman who was forcing him to go through this.

Because he wanted Jasmine to be a mother for Rafiq, and he wanted her now. He didn't know why he hadn't thought of asking her to marry him before, but the truth was it hadn't occurred to him until he'd needed to wed for the coronation.

He wanted Rafiq to have a mother, but not just any mother. He'd convinced his old nanny to come out of retirement to take care of his son, and he knew that his boy was in good hands with her. Loving hands. But Kalila was getting old and he felt guilty taking her away from her retirement.

Still, Adan was there every night, spending time with his son, playing with him, reading to him. Rafiq was loved in a way that Adan never had been. His own father had loved him, but he was a proud man incapable of showing true affection to his sons. They were meant to be hard men of the desert, not cosseted young men with a sense of entitlement.

But Adan didn't believe Rafiq would be any less manly because his father loved him and wanted him to be happy. There was nothing on this earth better than walking into the nursery each night and seeing that little face light up with the purest love he'd ever seen.

Isabella had claimed to love him once. He hadn't made that up, though she believed he had. He could still remember her saying it, after they'd made love one night. She'd been so young, so naive, and he'd pulled away from her, troubled. He didn't know why.

Shortly after that, she'd learned she was pregnant. And then the morning sickness took over and he'd left her bed. He'd wanted her to rest, to be healthy, and he'd felt as if his presence disturbed her sleep.

Adan frowned. Had he told her why he'd stopped sleeping with her? Of course she'd known why they weren't having sex—she'd been too ill to want it anyway—but had she realized why he'd left her alone in her bed?

It bothered him to think he hadn't. But what difference would it have made?

The psychiatrist he'd had examine her upon their arrival today could tell him nothing he didn't already know. Isabella claimed to have no memory of her marriage or of her baby. It was an unusual case, but not impossible. In consulting Isabella's records, the doctor had frowned and said that she had shown signs of postnatal depression, though her symptoms hadn't been abnormal at the time.

Baby blues were common enough, he'd said, and resulted from the changing hormones in a woman's body. Sometimes, the depression got worse and could cause hallucinations or thoughts of harming oneself or one's baby.

Adan had been shocked. He hadn't realized that anything could be wrong with Isabella at the time. Then the doctor suggested that she might have tried to commit suicide. Her records up to her disappearance showed no antidepressant usage. If her doctor at the time had believed she was suffering from postnatal depression, he should have prescribed medication to mitigate it.

It was possible, too, that her doctor simply hadn't recognized the signs. And Isabella would have been more vulnerable to the effect of the hormones on her body without them.

Adan didn't quite know what to make of all the information, but as he reached the nursery, he firmly shoved thoughts of Isabella aside. All he wanted right now was to hold his son and spend time watching his toddler antics. Adan pushed open the door and went into the suite of rooms that was overflowing with toys and games.

"Kalila," he called, but no one answered. He went into the nursery itself, but Rafiq was not in his crib or playing on the floor.

He checked his watch. Kalila and Rafiq were usually here at this time of day. He stood for some moments, wondering, until, like a bolt of lightning, a thought shafted through him.

A terrible thought.

He'd had Isabella put as far from here as he could get her, yet these were still the family quarters and her rooms weren't on another planet. They were simply down another corridor. He'd stationed a servant to make sure she didn't leave her room, so it should not be possible that she'd somehow found Rafiq.

And yet he suddenly feared, with a terrible, dreadful certainty that ate a hole in his gut and sent him running down the corridors to her room, that it was possible. As he skidded to a stop at her door, the man he'd stationed there fell off his chair and began to babble, his face pressed to the floor.

Adan could hear singing. She was singing, the sound so rich and pure it wrapped around him like a warm blanket on a cold desert night. He shoved open the door, his heart beating so fast as he prayed he was wrong, that he'd got the time mixed up, that his intuition was merely superstition—

She sat on one of the low couches, her eyes closed as she found the note and held it. Kalila perched on another sofa, across from Isabella.

And Rafiq stood with his hands on Isabella's knees, his little face turned up to hers as she sang. Adan's world went red. Rage curled and twisted inside him like a coiling snake.

The rage he understood, but there was another feeling underpinning it. Loss?

How could he feel loss? Rafiq was his, no matter what. This was one moment, one regrettable moment, and it would not be repeated. Rafiq would not remember it. Ever.

She let the note go and opened her eyes to smile down at Rafiq. He bounced in place, laughing in delight.

Isabella finished the song and held her arms out. Rafiq stretched his up until she bent and caught him. And then she was holding him close and Adan was dying inside.

"What is going on here?" he said smoothly, despite the churning emotion inside him.

All eyes turned to him. Kalila climbed to her feet and curtseyed. He hated that she did so, but she'd always been particular about observing the forms with him. As she would be with Rafiq, as well. A mother, but not a mother.

Isabella stood. Rafiq had his arms around her neck. When he saw Adan, he crowed, "Papa! Sing, Papa!"

"Does your papa sing?" Isabella asked.

Rafiq nodded his little head.

"Put him down," Adan growled. He thought she would argue with him, but she simply bent to set Rafiq on the floor. He held on to her neck and refused to let go.

"No want down!"

His expression was militant and Adan knew he was fighting a losing battle. Somehow he found the ability to move again. He walked over to Isabella and held his arms out.

"Come to Papa," he said, and Rafiq stretched his arms wide. Relief flooded him. Isabella let the boy go easily enough, but he didn't miss the way her fingers tightened oh so briefly before relinquishing his son.

He had to stand close to her to take Rafiq, and now his senses were overwhelmed with her scent. She'd showered and changed again since they'd arrived. Her hair was every bit as wild as it had been back in Hawaii, and it smelled like tropical flowers. He wanted to close his eyes and breathe her in.

Instead, he turned away. "Come, Kalila. It is time we took Rafiq for his *b-a-t-h* and bedtime."

Isabella did not want them to go, and yet she knew there was nothing she could do to stop Adan from taking Rafiq away. She'd spent the past hour singing for her baby, delighting in his little smile and enthusiastic singing along with her. Nothing had cracked a memory open in her head, but she'd felt as though everything was right with the world in the short time she'd spent with her son.

She did not want it to end. She felt whole when he was near. It was not a feeling she was accustomed to.

She also felt lost, she had to admit, because she didn't automatically know what to do or say to him. Just because he was hers didn't mean she understood him. It saddened her that she didn't know how to be a mother, but she desperately wanted to learn.

And Adan wanted to keep her from learning. He wanted to keep Rafiq away from her. When he'd spoken and she'd looked up to see him standing there, the hatred and rage on his face was worse than anything she'd seen yet. He did not believe she had value of any kind for their son, and it hurt her at the same time as it strengthened her resolve not to give up.

But she understood why he was cautious. How could she not after meeting that precious little child? Adan's primary goal was to protect Rafiq. She couldn't argue with that. But she could argue that he wasn't being fair, that she deserved a chance to be a part of her son's life just as he deserved a chance to know his real mother.

"Adan," she said.

She didn't think he would stop, but when Rafiq said, "Lady sing, Papa," Adan stopped short of the door.

"Not now, Rafi. The lady needs to rest."

"Lady sing!" he insisted.

"No, Rafi," Adan said—and Rafiq's face screwed up in a frown. She knew what was coming next, even in so short a time of knowing her son. He burst into tears, his face turning red as he wailed.

Adan shot her a look over the top of Rafiq's head that was full of loathing before he disappeared through the door. Kalila followed, and the servant reached in and shut the door behind them.

Isabella stood in the center of her lonely room, listening to Rafiq's wails as they disappeared down the hall. She was numb. Whereas just a few moments before she'd been full of life, she now felt drained and dull.

The laughter was gone. The warmth. The love.

She pressed her fist to her mouth, chewing on the knuckles. She loved Rafiq. It had happened that quickly. Instantly. She'd fallen head over heels for her little boy.

Her poor little motherless boy.

What had she done two years ago? Why? Why had she left him in the first place?

As hard as she tried, she couldn't remember anything about that time. It was blank, as blank as it had always been. She'd awakened and been told about the accident. Then she'd gone to her mother's to recover. That was all she could recall.

The doctor she'd spoken with today had merely shrugged and said that the brain was a strange and sensitive organ. What had happened to her was not common, but her memory loss wasn't completely unexpected, either. When she'd asked if she would ever remember, he'd said it was possible, though perhaps not likely.

Another hour passed before a servant brought her dinner. She ate alone, then took her coffee and went out onto the balcony that overlooked the gardens below. The sun had set recently, so the heat was finally leaching out of the air. The sky was red-tinted—almost like Hawaii, and yet not—and the Arabian Sea slid to dark purple in the glow of the sky.

Port Jahfar glittered like a jewel in the dusk. Industrial ships crowded the harbor in the distance, bringing supplies to the kingdom or taking on loads meant for other destinations. Her father had a home along the coast, much farther from here, where the turquoise water caressed the white shore. She'd loved that home growing up most of all. It was why she'd been drawn to Hawaii.

As she drank her coffee, the night darkened, the red fading away until it was only a ribbon along the horizon. And then she sensed that she was no longer alone. She knew who it was without turning to acknowledge him.

"Come to shove me off the balcony and end your troubles, Adan?" she asked.

Behind her, he blew out a breath. "No."

She heard him move, and then he was standing beside her. He'd changed into a dark polo shirt and jeans. His head was free of the *keffiyeh*. She wasn't certain what disconcerted her more—his handsome face framed in the dark cloth, or the added distraction of his hair and the shape of his head to accompany his chiseled features.

How was it possible to forget a man like this? To forget making love with him, sleeping and waking with him, eating with him, talking with him?

"He cried for over an hour," Adan said without preamble. She could hear the emotion in his voice, the love he felt for his son. It was the only thing about him that made him redeemable to her. Adan truly loved Rafiq, and everything he did was for Rafiq's well-being. Understanding that didn't make it any easier, however.

"I'm sorry," she replied, a lump rising in her throat at the thought of her baby crying.

"He refused to eat because he was so upset. Kalila finally got him to sleep." He shoved a hand through his hair. "I don't know how she did it."

He turned to her, propping his elbow against the railing. It was a casual gesture, and yet everything about his presence was anything but casual. There was tension in the lines of his body, tension in the furrow of his brow and the intensity of his gaze.

"It's not easy raising a child," he continued. "They are fussy, independent, messy and a million other things you can't imagine one tiny person could be. It's a giant responsibility."

"I know that, Adan." Her heart thrummed at his nearness, at the way he stood so close to her and discussed their child. It was as if, for a moment at least, they were on the same side. As if they were two parents talking about their son.

She knew better, however.

He pushed a hand through his hair. She found herself wanting to smooth the crisp curls back into place, but she did not do so.

"He does not know you," he said. "If you insert yourself into his life, and then decide you can't handle the responsibility, you will hurt him because he will have grown close to you."

She gripped the coffee cup in her fingers. "I didn't do anything wrong. I didn't try to be anything to him—"

"I know." He let out a sharp breath. "Kalila told me what happened. She was taking a shortcut back to the nursery when he heard you singing."

Her temper sharpened. "Then why are you here, if not to chastise me? I know you would be happier if I didn't exist. But I do, Adan. And I want to know my child."

His eyes glittered hotly in the westering light. His mouth tightened. Her gaze settled on those firm, sensual lips. They'd been so masterful against her own. The wetness flowing into her inner core at the thought shocked her. She was angry with him, and yet her body reacted to him until the tingle of desire was soon a buzz in her veins.

How could she feel this way for him? How could she be attracted to him when he infuriated her so much? Was her body remembering what her mind had forgotten?

He took a step closer, then stopped as if he realized

he'd done so against his will. His voice, when he spoke, was low and determined.

"I am here, Isabella, because I have come to a decision."

CHAPTER SIX

ADAN was taking a risk. He knew it, and yet he was now convinced it was the only solution. When he'd carried Rafiq back to the nursery, the child crying all the way because he wanted the lady to sing for him, Adan had realized that he could not undo what had been done.

Not only that, but perhaps he'd been wrong to try and keep Isabella away from Rafiq.

Not because he believed she was suddenly going to make a fabulous mother. He wouldn't bet Rafiq's future on that shaky hypothesis. But, his son was still so young, and he would encounter various people who would be a part of his life for a short while before they were gone again. Teachers. Friends. Even Kalila, who suffered from arthritis that would soon make taking care of Rafiq more difficult as he grew bigger and heavier.

People moved on. It happened all the time, and Adan couldn't protect Rafiq from it.

Isabella was looking up at him, her green eyes so wary and sad at the same time. She held her saucer in her right hand, the fingers of her left hooked through the coffee cup that she hadn't drunk from since he'd joined her.

She still smelled like tropical flowers. Tropical flowers, coffee and the spicy sweetness of the cardamom seed that flavored the brew. He wondered if she would taste sweet and spicy if he kissed her.

"What is it, Adan?" she asked, her voice as smoky and rich as the coffee. He shook thoughts of kissing her from his head.

"I'm going to give you two weeks with us." Because he'd decided that the only way to convince her she was not cut out for motherhood was to let her spend time with Rafiq. She'd walked away before—for whatever reason—and she would do so again.

And he intended that she know it sooner rather than later.

She seemed so serene, and yet he hadn't missed the tiny gasp that had escaped her.

"Two weeks," he repeated firmly. "But you are not to tell him you are his mother. He does not need the confusion."

"But I *am* his mother," she said.

"That's the deal, Isabella. Take it or leave it."

She tilted her head. "What am I supposed to be to him, then?"

Adan shrugged. "A nanny. A caretaker. A teacher. Someone who will not be staying."

She set the coffee down on a nearby table. The delicate china rattled as she did so, betraying her nerves. Or maybe it was anger. He had to acknowledge that she was certainly capable of bypassing nerves and going straight for the anger.

"And what happens at the end of two weeks?"

"We'll decide when we get there." It was all he could say to her. Because if he told her that he hoped to be divorced from her at the end of two weeks, she would most certainly fight him.

But it's what he expected. Two weeks for her to decide she didn't want to be a mother after all, and she would agree to a divorce, assuming his solicitor hadn't managed to get the job done by then. The coronation wasn't scheduled for another two weeks anyway, because the laws of Jahfar required a minimum twenty-one-day period of mourning before a new king was officially crowned.

She bowed her head, as if she were thinking. Her arms crossed beneath her breasts, and an arrow of heat sizzled into his groin at the way they nearly spilled over her silky tank top. When she lifted her head again, her eyes speared into him.

"You know I'm going to accept. What choice do I have? I'll do anything to spend time with my baby. And, whether you believe it or not, I care about his welfare every bit as much as you do. I won't tell him I'm his mother."

He inclined his head. "Thank you."

"It's not for you," she snapped. "It's for Rafiq. Because you're right, he doesn't need the confusion right now. He's too young to understand what it means, and I won't use him as a pawn in our argument with each other. Until we settle our issues, his understanding of who is who in his life should remain the same."

She was so different than she'd once been. The woman before him now lit up like a firecracker, blazing sparks of outrage and righteousness, whereas the woman she'd been before would have nodded meekly, accepting whatever decree he cared to make.

Like Jasmine, he thought. *No.* Jasmine was perfect,

nothing like Isabella used to be—and nothing like her now. Jasmine would not blaze in the night. She would glow softly. She would not defy him.

But there would be no need, would there? He and Jasmine were friends. There was no reason for sparks between them.

"Very well," he said, "tomorrow we are moving inland, to the Butterfly Palace. There are fewer people there, as well as fewer questions."

Because it was best if her return to Jahfar wasn't widely known. His staff knew, of course, but they were discreet and loyal. He had so little privacy anymore, but this was one area in which he meant to keep his— their—personal business confidential. He and Isabella would not play out the last days of their marriage before the public eye.

She seemed to understand, as she only nodded.

"Adan," she said when he turned to go.

He stopped. "Yes?"

"I want to speak with my father." She bit her lip, that lush lower lip he wanted to nibble as he thrust deep inside her body. The image of him doing just that started the telltale tingle at the base of his spine. He clamped down on his libido before he embarrassed himself. *Focus.*

He could *not* keep thinking of her that way. It was counterproductive to his plans.

"He's the only one who knows the truth about what happened," she continued.

A wave of frustration rolled through him then. He very much wanted to speak to Hassan Maro, as well. He wanted to know the truth. "Your father is out of the country."

She seemed to sink in on herself then, her shoulders slumping, the fire inside her flickering dangerously. One breath, he thought, and it would go out.

"It figures." She sighed.

He suddenly found himself wanting to pull her into his arms and comfort her. But he would not. He couldn't afford to soften toward her, couldn't allow his judgment to be clouded or to make her think something more was possible between them.

Then why are you taking her to the Butterfly Palace and letting her spend time with Rafiq?

Because he had to get her to agree to a divorce. That was it, the only reason—aside from the issue of keeping her return a secret from the public, of course. They would be isolated, but he would have plenty to keep him busy. He had a nation to run. He would never be alone with her. Kalila would be there, and Mahmoud, as well as a small staff.

He would spend time with her and Rafiq during the day. At night, they would go to separate rooms. It was a good plan. A sound plan.

"I have left orders that he is to be brought to me the moment he returns," he said. "It is the best I can do."

She tilted her chin up as her strength returned. "Fine. And now, if you don't mind, I think I'll go to bed. It's been a long day."

"Of course," he said, sweeping his arm wide to indicate that she precede him inside. She didn't stop once indoors, marching straight to the hall door and holding it open for him. It wasn't until he was halfway back to his own room that he realized he'd just been dismissed.

Early the next morning, a team of tailors and their assistants arrived. Isabella had just finished breakfast when the knock on her door sounded. A moment later, a servant led the procession into the outer rooms of her suite.

"His Excellency says you are to have a new wardrobe, my lady," the head tailor offered by way of explanation.

The morning was filled with measurements, choosing from bright bolts of silk georgette, and standing still for fittings of a few readymade items the women had brought along. Isabella felt self-conscious. She wanted to protest that she did not need so much, but the truth was she had no idea whether she did. Adan had said two weeks, but of course she hoped for more. The clothing she'd brought with her wouldn't get her through much more than a week.

She already missed her life in Hawaii, and yet she missed it the way you miss something that happened in the past—not as if it was something she desired now. Because now that she'd met her baby, she couldn't imagine anywhere else she wanted to be.

She did not know how they would work this out between them, but she hoped to be a part of Rafiq's life for far longer than two weeks. She sensed this was a test and, as much as it infuriated her to have to take it, she was determined not to fail.

By the time Adan came for her later that afternoon, she had a suitcase full of clothes to take along. She'd dressed in a soft green *abaya* for the trip by car into the desert. The garment skimmed her form, suggesting curves rather than delineating them.

Adan stopped short when he entered the room and she stood up. His eyes slid over her appreciatively, but he banked the fire in them as he met her gaze.

"You are ready, then?"

"Yes," she replied, as coolly as she could manage.

The ride to the Butterfly Palace took just over two hours in the caravan of Land Rovers that rolled up and down giant red sand dunes. The desert was stark and beautiful, and yet it made her heart beat crazily in her chest.

Was it because she had walked into the desert alone, as Adan said? Whatever had happened to her had happened out here. And that made her nervous.

She sat stiffly in the seat beside Adan, her hands clasped together in her lap. She'd wanted to ride with Rafiq and Kalila, but there hadn't been enough room in their car.

"Why is it called the Butterfly Palace?" she blurted after they'd rolled down yet another steep dune. Beads of sweat broke out on her brow and between her breasts. The car was air-conditioned, but it wasn't cool enough to conquer the evidence of her nerves.

Adan glanced over at her. "It was built five hundred years ago for the favorite wife of a king. She loved butterflies and had a garden built for them. In the spring, it was said, hundreds of butterflies swarmed the palace. They perched on her shoulders and hair, ate with her and even slept with her. And when her husband eventually died and she was brokenhearted, the butterflies carried her to heaven to be with him—or so the legend goes."

"Are there any butterflies there now?" she asked, trying to imagine the sad queen and her colorful companions.

"I have never seen any," he said. "I think the climate has shifted as the desert has grown, and it's now too hot for them here. There are butterflies closer to the sea, of course." He frowned and leaned closer to her. "Are you unwell, *habibti*? Do you need your headache medicine?"

Isabella swallowed against the tidal wave of nausea that threatened to take her down if she didn't hold fast against it. "It's not my head," she forced out. Tears pricked the backs of her eyes. "It's just so hot."

Adan's frown deepened. He pressed a button and gave an order to the driver in the front seat, and the blast of air from the AC unit intensified. He picked up a stack of papers he'd been leafing through earlier and fanned her with them.

Isabella closed her eyes and leaned back against the seat. "Thank you," she whispered.

"What is truly wrong, Isabella?"

His voice was soothing, and she had a sudden feeling that she needed to share it with someone. That maybe if she voiced her concerns, heard how silly they were, the feeling would go away. "It's the desert. I…feel…as if it's going to crush me beneath it."

She heard him sigh, and then she felt his arm around her, pulling her close against him. He continued to fan her with the papers. "You are safe with me," he said in a low voice. "I promise you that."

She sat stiffly at first, but the rhythm of the Land Rover, the soft breeze from the papers and the warm body at her side lulled her into a doze. She drifted in that half-twilight state between dreaming and waking. She thought of her father's house near the sea, then the one on the edge of the wildest part of Jahfar. Her father and mother rose up in her mind, arguing, of course, and then quickly faded away.

Then a man appeared before her.

A dark, dangerous man. Adan. He held his hand out and she slipped hers inside it. He pulled her to him and kissed her. She was wearing a deep orange *abaya*, heavily jeweled, and a veil covered her head. She was nervous, but he comforted her with soft words as he gently slipped the clothing from her body. Then he laid her on a bed and stripped off his clothes before lying down beside her.

She knew what came next as she gazed up into his face. That handsome face that had been so aloof all day, but was now intense and sensual. He caressed and kissed his way down her body, taking his time. He dipped his tongue into the wet seam between her legs and brought her to shattering bliss while she moaned and cried his name. Then he was on top of her, pushing at her entrance as the remnants of her pleasure ricocheted through her body.

As he pushed inside her, whispering hot words, she gasped out in pain and surprise—

Isabella blinked. The sun was bright and hot outside the car. Red sand spread as far as the eye could see in every direction. Beside her, Adan was frowning at her again.

"What is the matter, Isabella?"

Her body was hot, but not from fear this time. Oh, dear God. She'd been having an erotic dream about him—or was it a memory? She'd been wearing the dress from their wedding photo in the paper.

"I…" She swallowed. "I think I remembered something…with you."

His gaze sharpened. "You did?"

Isabella felt a fresh wave of heat wash over her. Why

had she told him that? Because now he'd want to know *what* the memory was.

On the other hand, what did it matter? Her desire to know if it was really a memory outweighed her embarrassment over the subject.

"I think it was our wedding night. I was wearing the dress from the photo. You undressed me before... before...your mouth... And then—"

Isabella closed her eyes. Dear God. Could it get any worse?

When she found the courage to peek at him, he was staring at her. His expression seemed distant, as if he, too, were thinking of that night.

Then he shook his head. "It's never going to work," he said more to himself than to her.

"What isn't?" Fear threaded through her voice, pitching it higher. Was he planning to turn the caravan around and take her back to Port Jahfar? Was he reconsidering allowing her to spend time with Rafiq? Dammit, *why* had she said anything?

"Adan," she said. Demanded.

He looked at her again, his dark eyes hot and intense. And then he kissed her.

It shocked her to realize that his mouth on hers felt right. That the sweep of his tongue, the hot thrill sliding down her spine and the explosive current of sensation pooling in her belly were familiar and welcome.

Her feminine core, already flooded with heat and moisture from the memory, ached with need.

Her arms drifted around his neck as he spread one broad hand against the small of her back and pulled her into his body so that she was half lying on his lap.

Reaching down, he hooked an arm around her legs and lifted her the rest of the way into his lap.

Her buttocks nestled against the solid hardness of his masculinity. When she moved, he groaned low in his throat, a sexy sound that made her want to press her hand against him just to see if the sound would get better.

He cupped her breast, his thumb caressing her sensitive nipple, rubbing so lightly and so expertly she thought she would scream. Her nipples were hard, tight points, and her whole body was attuned to every agonizing caress.

"I want you," he growled against her lips—and then he was kissing her throat, her collarbone, before claiming her mouth again.

Isabella couldn't stop the moan that rose in her throat. She'd kissed one man in the two years that she'd thought she was a different person, and she'd pulled back immediately because it hadn't felt right.

This did.

Incredibly, amazingly right. Which disconcerted her, because she had no illusions about Adan. He might want her physically, but he despised her. Perhaps he'd always despised her. Perhaps that's why she'd felt compelled to leave.

Feelings swirled in her head, her heart, until she couldn't untangle them. She felt happy—and sad. She felt cherished—and despised. She felt, with a certainty, that she had once loved him—but that he had not loved her. Sorrow rose up in a solid wave inside her and she suddenly put her hands against his chest and pushed.

It was too much.

He broke the kiss, confusion in his dark eyes as he

gazed down at her. His mouth—that beautiful mouth—was slick from kissing her, and she instantly wanted to press her lips to his again and forget her tangled thoughts.

"I—I'm not ready for this," she said, her voice thready. "It's too soon."

His expression cleared by degrees until he was once more the cool, unflappable ruler. He set her away from him and she smoothed her skirts self-consciously.

"You are correct, of course," he said. "Forgive me."

"It's not that I don't want…" Isabella swallowed. How could she say it? How could she admit that she did want him? It would be an acknowledgment of his power over her.

And she couldn't give him any more power than he already had.

"I don't know you well enough," she said softly. "I know we've had a child together, but what kind of man are you really? What kind of marriage did we have? Did we at least like each other?"

He leaned back on the seat and sighed. "We were good in bed," he said matter-of-factly. "Though we did not have much time together."

"Because you were so busy? Or do you mean because I got pregnant?"

"Both, I think. But mostly because you were ill during the pregnancy. We had one month, Isabella, before we began to live like roommates instead of lovers."

"Oh. Was it a difficult pregnancy, then?"

"Other than your nausea, no. Everything was normal."

She smoothed the fabric on her thighs again. "I wish I could remember. I feel…cheated."

Cheated because she'd carried her child for nine months and she could remember nothing about the experience. Cheated because she'd obviously shared her life—and body—with this man, and he was still a stranger to her.

Adan sighed. "You were very beautiful, in spite of your sickness. And you grew quite large. Rafiq weighed over nine pounds when he was born."

Isabella's jaw dropped. "He did? My goodness." And then she giggled, though it threatened to turn into a sob. She pressed her hand to her lips to stop it from doing so. "Maybe it's a good thing I don't remember."

Adan smiled. Her heart stopped. He was breathtaking when he did so. His face, already so handsome, became warm and open, almost innocent in a way. It was an odd thing to think about so hard a man, and yet it was the one word that popped into her mind. *Innocent.*

"You looked as if you'd swallowed three soccer balls," he said. "The doctor said it was only one baby in there, but I began to think he was wrong."

"Were you there when he was born?"

He shook his head and her heart sank a little at the sad expression on his face. "I was out of the country on business. You weren't due for another two weeks."

"I'm sorry you missed it, then."

He picked up her hand and kissed it. Shock raced in hot spirals along her nerve endings. "I am, too. I would have liked to have been there for you both. You had a difficult time with the labor and delivery, but Rafiq was healthy and you bounced back…"

His voice trailed off and she looked at him quizzically. "What, Adan?"

He shook his head. "Nothing. It's nothing."

"I *want* to remember," she said. "Even the hard parts. I want to remember every moment of our lives together. It's hard not knowing."

"Perhaps you will remember someday. You remembered our wedding night, after all."

"Did I? Or was it only a dream?"

One corner of his mouth quirked in a wicked grin. "No, you remembered it quite well. It was a long and pleasurable night."

Her heart pounded for an entirely different reason now. He was as tempting as sin. And she desperately wanted to take a bite out of the apple.

"Careful, Isabella," he growled suddenly. Except it wasn't an angry growl at all.

It was a passionate, sensual sound that stroked along her senses like a trail of hot candle wax.

"I don't understand," she managed.

He cupped a hand behind her head and pulled her in for a kiss. Just as quickly, he let her go again. "I'm a man, *habibti*, not a saint. If you keep looking at me like that, you're going to know me *very* well before we ever leave this car."

CHAPTER SEVEN

THE Butterfly Palace wasn't as ornate as she'd expected it to be. Nor was it anywhere near as big as the palace in Port Jahfar. Other than a caretaker and a housekeeper, there was no permanent staff. That was why, Isabella thought, they'd traveled in a caravan.

They still hadn't brought that many people along. A cook. Adan's assistant, as well as two extra office personnel. Two additional women to help the housekeeper and cook, and a couple of others whose functions she did not know.

Adan took a sleeping Rafiq from Kalila and carried him to his room, which was already prepared, while the housekeeper showed Isabella to her room. She wanted to go with Adan and Rafiq, but she told herself to be patient. They'd just arrived, and there was time to settle in. Besides, Rafiq was asleep and wouldn't even know she was there.

The room she was shown to was just a room, not a suite, but it was large and airy with tall ceilings, overstuffed couches, and an inlaid wooden armoire and dressing table. A large canopied bed occupied one wall, the mattress thick and covered with a cream duvet and a collection of pillows.

White curtains hung on either side of distressed wooden doors that opened to the outside. The doors were old and shuttered to let the light in, but glass had been fitted to the outer portion of the casement, so that the doors could be opened at any time and yet the room would remain cool due to the modern air-conditioning that had been added to the palace.

The doors were pushed partially to, but Isabella didn't open them to see what was outside. First, she wanted to unpack, and then she would explore.

While she was putting everything away, a maid brought refreshments—mint tea and a selection of cool fruit—and then hurried away again before Isabella could tell her she really didn't need anything.

"Is it to your liking?"

Isabella whirled at the sound of his voice. They'd only arrived a little over a half an hour ago—how could she already be so pleased to see him, as if they'd been separated for days instead of minutes?

"It's lovely," she replied.

Adan strode over and pulled open the wooden doors. "Come, let me show you something."

He held out his hand. She didn't even hesitate before joining him and slipping her hand into his, her skin sizzling where they touched. He stared down at her for a moment, as if he, too, were jolted by the contact, and then he was pushing open the glass and leading her onto a shadowed terrace.

Bougainvillea vines grew in profusion over the arbor that stretched the length of the terrace. A short sandstone wall ran along the back of the terrace, and beyond that was a small hedge that seemed to wind in a path, though she couldn't figure out the pattern.

"It's a labyrinth," Adan said, tugging her forward. "The Butterfly Queen had it built centuries ago. The original hedge didn't survive, but this one follows the path she had laid out."

They stopped at the entrance to the labyrinth. She could see the path meandering back and forth.

"You can see all the way to the center," she said. "I didn't think that's how it worked."

He grinned, and for the second—third?—time today, her heart went into free fall. "You're thinking of a maze," he said. "Two different things. A labyrinth is for meditation, among other things. The idea is to walk it and see what the path shows you. It's a personal journey, and it means something different for everyone."

She'd have never thought he was the meditating type. "Do you walk it?"

"I have."

"And?"

Again, with the smile. "Truthfully, I didn't get it the first time. I was impatient and wanted to reach the end. And then I realized that impatience is one of my faults, and the labyrinth could perhaps teach me something after all."

"Nooo," Isabella said disbelievingly. "Don't tell me you have faults. I can't imagine that to be true."

He laughed. "It's possible I have one or two."

Isabella grinned back at him. "Careful, Adan, or I might have to start liking you after all."

"I'll be sure to do something evil just to keep you on your toes," he replied.

She looked out over the labyrinth and the garden beyond and sighed. The sun was setting now, and everything was bathed in a soft ocher glow. It was peaceful.

So much quieter than Port Jahfar—or even Maui, with the tourists and the parties taking place so frequently along the beach.

"Did we talk like this before?" she asked. "Or did I merely bow my head and do or say whatever I thought you wanted?"

His fingers ghosted along her cheek, pushed her riot of golden hair away from her face. Her heart raced at the soft touch of his skin on hers. She had to stop this. Because every time he touched her or smiled at her, her heart opened just a little bit wider for him.

"You already know what the answer is, Isabella, even if you cannot remember it."

She looked up at him. His dark eyes regarded her with something that she thought might be appreciation. Not sexual appreciation, though there was that, too, but an intellectual approval that she was certain she'd not had from him when they were first married.

"Yes, I do. I did what I'd been raised to do, Adan. What my father expected from me. What you expected from me. I tried to be a good Jahfaran wife. I know that, even if I have no memory of it."

"And what would you do now?" he asked. "If the clock was rewound and you went into our marriage as the person you are at this moment?"

She bit her lip. Why was he asking her this? Was he fishing for an answer, trying to gauge her suitability to be his wife? If she said the right thing, did it mean she could stay with Rafiq forever?

She opened her mouth to say what she thought he wanted to hear.

And then she stopped.

She couldn't do it. She couldn't say what she thought

the correct answer was, because it wasn't what she knew to be true for herself. Was she still that girl who'd tried so desperately to please her feuding parents? Who'd said whatever they'd wanted to hear if only it would make them happy with her?

She wasn't, and she couldn't ever be again.

Isabella took a deep breath. It was filled with the fragrance of bougainvillea and the spicy scent of the man standing so near.

"I would be me, regardless of whether it pleased you or not," she said.

His smile was as sudden and unexpected as diamonds raining down from heaven. "I am very glad to hear it."

Dinner was served picnic-style, on a big mat under the stars in the garden with gas lanterns to light the night. There was tabbouleh salad, fresh hummus, roasted lamb with lemon and garlic, rice, and a variety of olives, cheeses, mangoes, figs and fresh hot flat bread that tasted amazing with everything.

Isabella sighed as she popped a bite of bread in her mouth. Rafiq sat beside her, his little head tilted up to watch her eat.

"Very good," she said. "Yummm. Does Rafi want a bite?"

He shook his head—but then he nodded, and Isabella laughed as she tore off a small piece of bread and fed it to him. He chewed so seriously, then got up to toddle toward his father on the other side of the mat. They'd long ago learned to make a path down the center. Dishes were arrayed to either end of the mat with a big swath in the middle for Rafiq to hold court.

Kalila sat in a chair beside them. She'd insisted on joining them on the mat, but Adan had told her no. At first, Isabella had thought he meant to send her away, but he pulled a chair from nearby and perched it there for her.

Isabella's heart did that melty thing again when she watched him help the old woman into the chair. He truly cared for Kalila.

Now, Rafiq climbed into Adan's lap and began babbling something. Adan's forehead wrinkled as he listened intently. Then he picked Rafiq up and hugged him tight, tickling him as the little boy laughed and squirmed.

Isabella bit her lip. Emotion swirled through her in sharp currents. She was happy—and sad.

She was confused—and frustrated. Hopeful—and hopeless. So many emotions, so many possibilities.

"Sing, Papa!" Rafiq exclaimed through his giggles.

"Ah, you want Isabella to sing? Perhaps you should ask her."

Rafiq turned his head to look at her. He stuck a finger in his mouth, chewing on it while he watched her with dark eyes. His father's eyes. Both sets of eyes stared at her now, waiting.

"Ask her," Adan urged.

"Bell sing?"

Isabella's heart swelled with love. It was the first time he'd called her anything besides 'lady.' It was progress, and she was ridiculously pleased.

"Of course I'll sing for you, sweetheart," she said.

"Go sit with Isabella," Adan said, and Rafiq toddled his way to Isabella's side. Then he plopped down in front of her and fixed those sweet eyes on her.

She started with a soft, slow island tune she'd learned on Maui, then sang a couple of Jahfaran songs. Rafiq watched her, mesmerized, until eventually his eyes began to droop. Isabella smiled, but she didn't stop singing. As he tottered, she pulled him close and he settled against her lap. When she looked across at Adan, he was watching her intently. His eyes were as dark and hot as always, but for once she wasn't thinking of how he despised her so much as she was thinking of how it had felt to kiss him in the car today.

Of how he'd caressed her body and told her that he wanted her. Was it possible they could work their way through this? It seemed odd to be thinking it, when she'd so recently sworn to one of the waitresses at Ka Nui's that she would never spend her life with a man who didn't love her—

But that was before she'd realized she was already married and had a child with this man.

Her fingers combed through Rafiq's soft curls. She would do anything, sacrifice anything, for this child. It was the oddest sensation, and yet it was the absolute truth. She knew it to the bottom of her soul.

She sang more quietly now, as Rafiq's eyes remained closed and his breathing evened out. A few more minutes and Adan nodded at her. She let the last note taper off and then it was quiet, except for the sound of the gas flames in the lanterns and the night sounds of locusts. Occasionally, there was a distant howl from a lonely jaguar hunting the dunes.

Isabella glanced at Kalila, who was shifting in her chair, and realized that the woman was probably uncomfortable by now. As much as she would love to continue to sit here with Rafiq asleep on her lap, she couldn't let Kalila be stiff from sitting too long.

"Perhaps we should take him to bed," she suggested, glancing at Kalila when Adan looked at her.

"Yes, I think you are right." Then he got up and came to take Rafiq from her. They progressed into the house while a servant began to clean up the dishes. This time, Isabella followed Adan all the way to Rafiq's room. It was packed with toys, of course, and decorated in cool blues and white. Connected to his room was another, and this was where Kalila stayed. Adan told her to go ahead to bed, his voice full of concern and gentleness. She curtseyed before going into the room and shutting the door.

Isabella thought that Adan stiffened, but then she decided she must have imagined it because he turned and laid Rafiq so gently into his crib. His hand ghosted over Rafiq's curls, and then he bent and placed a kiss on his son's forehead.

Isabella's eyes filled with tears. Every man, no matter how hard, could be brought to his knees by something. For Adan, it was love for his son that made him human.

Adan stood and turned to her. "If you want to…"

She shook her head. She desperately wanted to kiss Rafiq goodnight, but she was afraid to disturb him. She didn't know how to do all the things she wanted to do just yet. It saddened and infuriated her all at once, but she had to be patient.

Adan took her hand and led her from the room and back out onto the terrace where coffee had been set at a small table for two. He pulled her chair out and she sank onto it, her pulse pounding in her throat and temples as he stood so close.

And then he was sitting across from her and lifting his coffee to his lips as he turned to gaze out at the darkened garden.

"It is very peaceful here," he said after a few moments of silence. "I would stay for weeks if it were possible."

"I imagine it's been very hectic since your uncle died."

"I have been the heir for over a year now, but yes, it has still been quite an adjustment. There is much to do when one is responsible for an entire nation."

"But we have a parliament now. Surely that helps."

"I think it does, yes. But there is still much work to be done. Fortunately, wherever I am, I am connected. Imagine the days before we had computers and cell phones."

"A trip out here would have been a true vacation then."

"Yes. Now, it is simply another stop. A different location, but the world does not truly go away."

It occurred to her that she didn't really know anything about him. "I'm sure I must have known this before, but how many siblings do you have?"

"Three brothers and one sister, who came much later in life. She is ten now."

"I always wanted a sister. Or a brother," Isabella added. She'd been so lonely, with her books and tutors and no other children to play with.

Adan seemed to know without asking what she meant. "I would like siblings for Rafiq, as well. He would enjoy having other children to play with."

Isabella studied the steaming liquid in her cup. "I'm surprised you didn't remarry by now."

He shrugged. "Time passed faster than I thought. I don't think I realized it had been two years until very recently."

"Do your brothers have children?"

"Not yet," he said. "Only one of them has married. The other two seem to think playing the carefree bachelor in Europe to be more fun." His eyes narrowed. "What about you, Isabella? Did you find playing the bachelorette fun?"

A shiver crept over her, not only because the sun had gone down and the desert was cooling. "I didn't date, if that's what you mean."

"Why not? You are a beautiful woman. And you must have got lonely."

Her heart throbbed. "Did you?"

His eyes glittered in the half-light of the torches. "Ah, answering a question with a question. Classic avoidance. And yes, I did get lonely."

"So did I. But I didn't date." She sighed and told him the truth. "It didn't feel right somehow. But I did let a man kiss me once."

He looked as if he could bite a nail in two. A fresh wave of irritation flooded her.

"It's not like I knew about you," she said. "And it was only a kiss. I'll bet you can't say the same," she added defiantly.

"I'll bet I can," he replied coolly. "I've kissed no one but you since the day we were married."

Her mouth dropped open. "I don't believe it."

He set the coffee down. "Believe it, Isabella. I've had

a child to raise and a business to run—and then I had a throne to prepare for. There's been no one but you."

She blinked in surprise. "But you were getting married again!"

"Jasmine is an old friend."

"I—I don't know what to say." She really didn't. A man like him...celibate?

"There is nothing to say." He stood abruptly. "Perhaps it's time we called it a night, yes? It's been a long journey and it's getting late."

She got to her feet, too. "What's the point in getting angry with me? It's not my fault."

"Nothing is, is it?"

She clenched her fists at her side. "What do you want from me, Adan? I'm trying."

"And I'm not?" he asked dangerously.

Isabella blew out a breath. "That's not what I meant. I meant this is hard, for both of us, and there's not a lot we can do about the past now."

"I'm beginning to think this was a bad idea after all," he said softly, his gaze dropping briefly to her lips before spearing her again.

"We just got here. You promised me two weeks."

"Promises, as you very well know, are easily broken," he said. And then he stalked into the house, leaving her lonely once more.

CHAPTER EIGHT

ADAN couldn't believe he'd told her. He'd confessed to
her that he'd had no lover since she'd gone away. It hadn't
been intentional. After she'd been declared dead, he'd
grieved her loss. But he hadn't been heartbroken because
of it. He'd grieved because she was Rafiq's mother, because he'd been fond of her.

He'd taken her presence in his life for granted, and
he'd regretted that immensely. But that wasn't what had
stopped him from attending to the sexual part of his life
after she was gone.

He'd always intended to take a mistress. Or another
wife. It had just never happened. He truly had been busy,
first with taking care of Rafiq and finding a decent
nanny for him. Adan had fired three nannies before
he'd finally begged Kalila to come raise his son.

After that, he'd been busy with his business interests
and then with the aftermath of his cousin's death and
becoming the heir to the throne. There'd been no time
in his life for casual affairs. He'd missed sex, missed
women, but he'd had little time to worry about it.

Now that he'd brought Isabella out here, all he could
think of was sex. He'd intended to stay busy and stay
away from her as much as possible. But then she'd told

him in the car about her memory of their wedding night, and he'd realized the futility of that plan.

He wanted her. And as he'd sat with her tonight and listened to her sing, as Rafiq had fallen asleep on her lap, he'd realized that his intention was to take her to his bed at the end of the evening. He'd pushed everything from his mind but her.

Then she'd told him she'd kissed another man. Until then, he'd purposely avoided thinking about what she'd been up to for the past two years as a lounge singer.

Hearing it had made him crazy. It was ridiculous, because it was nothing really, and yet the knowledge of that kiss had sliced into him with the utter unfairness of it. He'd been celibate, and she'd been kissing another man.

It was nothing, and everything.

He'd wanted to pick her up and carry her to his room that very minute. He'd wanted to make her his. Irrevocably.

But it was wrong—wanting her was wrong—because in two weeks, when this was all over, he would wed Jasmine.

It was late when he shoved the covers aside and got out of bed. His body was heated and his brain wouldn't settle down. He was restless, like a caged lion. He padded naked to the en suite bathroom, then pulled on a pair of shorts, not really certain what he intended to do other than leave the bedroom.

Outside the window, movement in the garden caught his eye. And then he realized what it was: Isabella walking the labyrinth by moonlight.

The path was dark, but the moon gave enough light to make out the pattern. Isabella moved slowly through the labyrinth, wondering when illumination was supposed to happen. She walked closer to the inside, and then farther away again. Just when she thought she was almost there, another twist in the pattern took her to the outside of the circle.

She didn't know why she was doing this. She lifted her head to look at the dark walls of the small palace. A light burned in an upper window, but that was all. The torches had been turned out hours ago, and the garden was dark and still.

She'd gone to bed and slept fitfully, her dreams filled with Adan and Rafiq—but mostly Adan. She'd dreamed of lying in bed with him, of telling him she loved him and of him stiffening beside her. Then she'd dreamed of waiting for him to come to her bed and falling asleep in tears when she realized he wasn't coming after all.

The dreams had disturbed her. She'd wanted to know their meaning. It was silly to think that walking a dark path in the moonlight was going to teach her anything, but she'd been drawn out here by the idea that it would calm her.

She wasn't feeling calm so much as frustrated, however.

"This is ridiculous," she muttered as another turn took her away from the center. Then she stopped in the pathway. This wasn't working. It would be better simply to go inside.

She turned to leave, intending to step over the knee-high hedges, but gasped at the sight of a man standing at the edge of the labyrinth, watching her.

Adan.

"I couldn't sleep," she said.

He stepped over the first hedge. "Neither could I."

Then he stepped over another one. "You aren't giving up, are you, Isabella?"

He wasn't wearing a shirt. Dear God in heaven. His torso gleamed in the moonlight, all hard planes and ridges where muscle and bone melded to create something damn near to perfection.

Isabella swallowed. No, not *near* perfection. Definitely perfection. She'd seen enough muscled chests on the beaches of Maui for the past year to know perfection when she saw it.

"I'm not getting anywhere," she said, her pulse beginning to throb in her throat. And elsewhere.

Her body was reacting, melting, aching. The surge of moisture between her legs didn't shock her. Adan made her feel things that no man ever had. Hot, needy things. She wanted to roll with him in a bed, to feel his magnificent body inside hers, to see if the things she'd dreamed—remembered?—were as good as they were in her head.

"It takes patience," he said, stepping over another hedge, and then another one.

"I've waited too long," she said—and wondered exactly what she meant by that statement. He stepped over the last hedge, stopping in front of her. He was so near, his body radiating so much heat that she thought she might burn if she touched him.

"Sometimes waiting makes the culmination that much sweeter." His deep voice was a vibration of sound through her body. She felt the words as much as she heard them. "Finish the path, Isabella."

"Will you go with me?" Because it seemed it would be easier if someone was with her. Less frustrating.

Slowly, he shook his head. "You have to walk it alone. But I'll be waiting in the center."

And then, before she could stop him, he hopped the rest of the hedges into the middle. She wanted to do the same. She stood there, undecided for several moments. It was just a path, for heaven's sake, and yet it intimidated her.

"Trust me, *habibti*. Walk the path," he urged.

Isabella blew out a breath and started to trace her way through the path again. She didn't want to finish. She wanted to *be* finished. Frustration built inside her like a snowball, gaining layers on each turn. The weight of it pushed outward until she felt she would split apart if she didn't reach the middle. It urged her to just hop the hedges and join him.

No.

She was going to walk the damn thing at least once. She would not allow him to call her a quitter. She wasn't a quitter, no matter what he might think. She didn't know why she'd left her father's house in the night, alone, but she would be damned if she'd let this man continue to believe it was because she had no staying power.

She'd be damned if she'd let *herself* think it was because she had no staying power. Because that was her secret fear, she acknowledged. That she was somehow flawed and that Adan had been right. That she'd left because she couldn't handle the responsibility.

She circled toward the center again, then back outside, and then, just when she thought she was about to be directed to the outside yet again, the pathway spilled her into the grassy center. She stopped abruptly as a flood of emotion nearly overwhelmed her. And then the feelings of unworthiness, guilt and fear lifted off her shoulders—as if she'd been carrying a load of rocks that had suddenly fallen away.

It was shocking. Because all she'd done was walk a circular, twisting path into a small clearing. It was nothing significant. Nothing earth-shaking or life-changing.

And yet she felt as if she'd succeeded somehow.

Adan held out his hand and she took it, let him pull her into the center of the clearing. He turned her until her back was to him. She could feel his body pressed close to hers, feel the heat and hardness of him. He was so solid, so overwhelming.

And he'd made love to no one but her in three years.

Isabella shivered. Why had she thought of that, out of everything she could possibly think of at this moment?

His lips touched her ear. "It's surprising how it makes you feel, isn't it?"

She could only nod.

His hands were on her shoulders, burning into her. Then one slipped down, curved around her midsection and pulled her tighter to his body. His arousal was unmistakable, pressing into the small of her back, and she closed her eyes and took a shuddering breath.

Suddenly, she knew why she was here. Why they were here together.

"Adan...I want..." She couldn't finish the sentence. A lump rose in her throat.

"I know," he replied. "It's inevitable. It has been inevitable since the moment I found you again."

She turned in his embrace then, tilting her head back to gaze up at him. His face was stark, as if he had been fighting his feelings and could do so no longer. As if he'd surrendered to something bigger than himself.

And she knew what it was. Desire. Lust. Need. Complete and total, as she'd never felt before.

Except that wasn't true, she realized. She had felt it before. For him. For Adan.

She ran her palms up his bare chest, glorying in the feel of hot naked skin, of the hard smooth planes of muscle and the shuddering tension coiled there.

He wrapped his arms around her body and pulled her in tight, his head lowering to claim her lips with his own.

Isabella sighed with the pure pleasure of his kiss. His tongue tangled with hers as if it had done so a thousand times. His hands came up to cup her face, and then he deepened the kiss. She responded immediately, instinctually, though she had no conscious knowledge of what to do.

Or did she?

She dropped one hand down his torso, slid her fingers along the waistband of his shorts. She was rewarded with a growl of pleasure. A rush of pure feminine power went to her head.

How many times had they kissed like this? How many times had she touched him exactly as she just had?

"We need to go inside," he said, lifting his head. "I am not prepared."

It took her a moment to figure out his meaning. "I'm on the pill," she replied. And then she almost wished she hadn't when he stiffened beneath her fingertips. "My cycles were irregular. The doctor said it would help regulate them."

She thought he might walk away then and there, but he hesitated only a moment before bending to kiss her again. Then he caught the bottom of her tank top in his fingers and slid it upward. She hadn't put on a bra to come out here, so when he reached the naked flesh of her breasts, he groaned before breaking the kiss and whipping the shirt over her head.

His broad hands wrapped around the soft mounds, his fingers tweaking her nipples gently. Isabella's breath caught at the riot of sensations streaking through her. She clutched his forearms to steady herself.

"You are beautiful, Isabella. Just as I remembered," he said. There was an edge to his voice, a sharp slice of—*something*—that called out to her and made her body flood with heat and moisture.

She was so ready for him. Ready for whatever he wanted from her.

"Adan," she gasped as his head dropped and he took one pouting nipple in his mouth. Her head fell back as he suckled her, his lips and teeth and tongue knowing exactly what to do in order to make that excruciating connection between her breast and her aching core. Every pull of his mouth on her nipple created an answering spike of pleasure in the wet crease between her legs. She ached for him, for his possession, in ways she hadn't ever dreamed were possible before now.

He stopped, and she cried out, reaching for him to keep him from stopping.

Adan laughed, a low, satisfied male sound that made her nerve endings prickle with heat. "Do not fear, Isabella. I'm nowhere near finished with you yet."

He made quick work of the zipper on her jeans, sliding them from her body and turning to place them on the ground with her top. Then he slipped out of his shorts and spread them out, as well.

Isabella's breath caught at the sight of him naked in the moonlight. His body was magnificent, every line and shadow of him hard and perfectly formed. His erection jutted from his body proudly, and she found herself aching to touch him. To take him inside her and know what it felt like to make love with him.

She went into his arms without hesitation, and he lowered her to the grass, placing her on top of the clothing. Around them, the hedges shut them in from prying eyes. Over top of them, stars blazoned across the sky in the billions while the moon gently lit the curves and hollows of their bodies.

Adan kissed her again, and she put her arms around him, holding him close as he slipped a hand between her legs and found her wet center.

His groan made her heart leap with joy. And then she couldn't think because his thumb slid over her clitoris. Again and again while her body tautened like a bow beneath his fingers.

When he stopped what he was doing, she murmured a protest, but he only laughed.

"It will get better, I promise," he said, and then he was kissing his way down her neck, her collarbone. He took his time with her breasts, licking and sucking until she was panting his name—and then he swiped his tongue down the center of her belly, dipping into the hollow of her belly button before teasing her bikini line with kisses.

Isabella held her breath as he parted her soft folds. They were slick and swollen and so sensitive that she trembled with the slightest caress of his breath across her skin.

And then his tongue dipped into her moistness and she arched off the ground in ecstasy.

"We've hardly begun," he murmured against her flesh. He slid his tongue the length of her, broadside, and then teased her clitoris with soft swirls that didn't quite do what she wanted.

But then he did do what she wanted, what she craved, as he licked and sucked and nibbled her until she flew apart much too quickly with a harsh cry. A single hot tear slipped down her cheek as she gasped with pleasure and surprise at the intensity of her release.

Had it always been like this between them? She wanted desperately to remember, and yet she couldn't. A trickle of memory here and there was all she'd been allowed, when what she wanted was for the floodgates to open and everything to come back.

He moved up her body then, his mouth tangling with hers once more as he gripped her buttocks in a broad hand and positioned her beneath him. She wrapped her legs around his waist, her whole body shaking as he began to push inside her.

"You must tell me if I hurt you," he said, his muscles corded with the tension of taking his time.

Isabella swallowed a gulp of fear. She wanted him so desperately, in spite of her release a few moments ago, and yet she was frightened of him, too. Frightened of what this would mean.

"I don't really know what to do," she confessed shamefully. "I'm trying."

He kissed her again. "You're doing everything right, *habibti*. Everything."

He moved forward relentlessly, and for a moment she thought he would be too much for her, that she would have to tell him to stop. Her fingers curled into his arms, her nails digging into him as he filled her.

And then her body opened to him as if it had always done so, and he slid the rest of the way home with a groan. He was so deeply inside her she could feel the pulse-beat of his body within hers.

He didn't move, and she gazed up at him in wonder and shock. Had it always felt this way? The amazing sense of fullness and anticipation sent little electrical charges across her skin until she was dying for him to move, to take her even higher.

How could she feel so much pleasure when he'd done nothing more than enter her body?

The look on his face was equally awed and bewildered. It was as if time stopped while they stared into each other's eyes, as if the world ceased to turn, and no one existed except the two of them.

I love you echoed inside her heart—but her head insisted it wasn't true. How could you love a man you'd forgotten, a man you hadn't yet gotten to know again?

You couldn't. It was simply the overwhelming emotions she felt at being joined with him this way.

"Isabella," he said softly, and his voice held a kind of amazement that she recognized. As if he too were blown away by feelings he couldn't explain.

Another tear dropped down her cheek. He caught it with a finger.

"It would be the hardest thing I have ever done, but if this hurts you, we can stop," he told her. "Pain should not be a part of this. Ever."

She couldn't tell him that pain was a part of it for her, but not physical pain. Never physical pain.

"No," she said quickly. "Oh, no. Don't stop, Adan. Please don't stop."

With a soft exclamation, he began to move inside her. He took his time at first. Her body instinctively knew his, knew the rhythm, and she rose to meet him as he withdrew again and again, his thrusts gaining power each time they met.

It didn't take long for their lovemaking to slip into the danger zone, to become something so hot and intense that they were no longer in control of it. At some point, their hands twined together on the ground above her head. Though it was cool in the garden, sweat slicked their bodies as they tangled together in the center of the labyrinth.

Everything Adan did, she realized, was designed to spin out her pleasure for as long as he could make it last. But it was inevitable that it had to end. Isabella caught the fine edge of the wave, and then plunged into the depths of a shattering release that had her sobbing his name as she shoved her hips upward to meet him.

Adan gripped her bottom in both hands, lifting her to him as he made her pleasure last and last and last. By the time it was over, she was wrung out, spun out, shattered beyond repair. She would never be the same again.

"Look at me, Isabella," he said.

Her eyes snapped open.

"I want to watch you come for me."

"I can't possibly—"

"Believe me, you can." And then he began to move again. For the barest second, she wanted to beg him to stop—it was too much, too intense, and she would never survive it a second time. When he'd brought her to orgasm with his mouth, it had been amazing and wonderful.

But this…this was earth-shattering not only to her body, but also to her soul.

And then, just like that, the feeling caught again, spinning up inside her in one long pleasurable wave that she could no more deny than she could stop breathing.

This time when she shattered, he went with her. He gripped her hips, holding her to him, and plunged deeply into her body, shuddering inside her with such force that he cried out sharply as he came.

Eventually he rolled to his side, taking her with him until he was on his back and she was lying on top of him. She laid her head against his damp chest, breathing harder than she would have believed possible, and closed her eyes.

His fingers traced up and down her spine, softly, rhythmically, until she felt herself drifting. They stayed like that until their bodies cooled and the night air sent a shiver tiptoeing across her.

"We should go in," Adan said. His voice sounded sleepy, as if he, too, had been drifting.

Isabella pushed herself up, yawning. "I need my clothes."

Adan got to his feet and helped her up. "Forget the clothes," he said. And then he swung her into his arms and carried her into the house.

CHAPTER NINE

ADAN woke sometime around dawn and reached for the woman in his bed. She came to him instantly, opened to him, and then he was stroking into her body and losing his sense of place, his sense of self, as he got lost inside her lush sensuality. He thrust into her with more force, more rawness, than he ever had before.

She'd been so naive and sweet when he'd married her. He would not have considered making love to her like this, riding her body hard, glorying in the answering urgency of her need. She drove him to this, drove him to want to possess her again and again.

He hadn't intended to take her to his bed. Hell, he hadn't intended to make love to her at all. When he'd gone outside earlier, it had been more out of curiosity than anything else. He hadn't thought they would end up naked and making frantic love in the center of the labyrinth.

But they had. And when it was time to come inside, he'd thought they would part ways when he carried her to her bed and left her there.

Except that he'd gone straight to his room instead. Once there, he'd been delighted when she'd wrapped her hand around him and let him know she was ready for another round. He'd lain on his back and thrust up inside her while she ground her hips against him, her beautiful breasts bouncing in the moonlight, her glorious hair tickling his chest when she leaned forward to suck one of his nipples.

Now, her breathy moans filled his ears, made him crazy. He took her lips, caught her moans in his mouth and gave them back to her when he exploded inside her a short time later.

Adan fell asleep again, his arms wrapped around the quivering, sighing woman beside him. When he awoke much later, light was streaming through the windows and across the bed—and he was alone.

He sat up, half wondering if it had all been a dream. But, no, his body could attest to the fact it had not. He showered and dressed, then went in search of food, coffee and Isabella.

He found her in the kitchen with Rafiq and Kalila. She carried Rafiq on her hip as she floated around the kitchen island, gathering ingredients from the refrigerator, and pots and pans from the hanging rack above. She looked beautiful, radiant, her entire body glowing with that special look of a well-pleasured woman.

She smiled when she looked up and saw him. "Look, Rafi, there's your daddy. Say hi to Daddy."

"Dada," Rafiq yelled.

Adan's heart twisted. He loved Rafiq so much, and yet he couldn't help the twinge of jealousy that stabbed into him while Isabella held their son. He should be pleased the boy liked her, and yet, part of him was not.

Adan stepped forward and held out his arms, gratified when Rafiq went straight into them. It was petty of him, he knew, and yet he was delighted his boy wanted him more than he wanted to stay with Isabella.

When he caught her eye, he was surprised to see that she didn't seem disappointed. In fact, she was smiling at him as if they shared a secret.

Which, he supposed, they did. She crooked an eyebrow, and he found himself thinking of last night—of her lips, her sighs, the catch in her throat, the feel of her sex surrounding him, of that warm, wet, amazing place he wanted to spend hours exploring.

He broke eye contact with her and kissed his son on the cheek. He needed to stop thinking about Isabella before he grew hard in the middle of the kitchen. Before he handed Rafiq to Kalila and dragged his wife—*his wife*—back to his bed for the rest of the morning.

"Did you sleep well, Your Excellency?" Isabella said teasingly.

"Not as well as I would've liked."

"I'm sorry to hear that. Perhaps you should get a new mattress or something."

"The mattress is fine," he said. "It just needs to be broken in a bit more. Rigorous bouncing might do it."

Her eyes widened as she looked at him. She glanced at Kalila, who seemed oblivious to the undercurrents as she worked a puzzle in a magazine. Adan grinned as Isabella cut her gaze back to him.

Rafiq bounced in his arms then. "Bell!" he exclaimed. "Bell, Bell, Bell!"

Bell indeed, Adan thought.

"Yes, baby boy?" Isabella said.

"Bell!"

Isabella laughed, the sound as sweet and pure as spring water. "I'm sorry to hear you did not sleep well,

Your Excellency. Perhaps you should return to bed and catch up on your rest. We wouldn't want you to be unable to, um…keep up, as it were…"

"I think I can manage," he said, shooting her a grin. "Especially if I get some breakfast. Who's in charge of cooking around here?"

Isabella smiled. "The cook is shopping at the local market for a few things. I am making breakfast."

"You can cook?"

Her green eyes were filled with humor. "I had to learn a thing or two recently. Cooking was one of them."

He was doubtful, but she set about scrambling eggs and making toast. Before he knew it, she'd plopped plates of food in front of him and Kalila. Kalila looked at the blackened edges of toast doubtfully.

"It's American," Adan said helpfully. Kalila cut her eyes at him while Isabella's back was turned. Adan shrugged. Then he picked up a fork and dug into the eggs. Kalila followed suit, though she looked apprehensive.

Isabella came around and took Rafiq, placing him in his high chair and giving him a plate of food, as well.

Adan popped the eggs into his mouth. His taste buds rebelled instantly. He would have spat the eggs out, but Isabella was watching him hopefully.

"Good, right?"

"Um…yes," he replied. The eggs weren't inedible so much as overcooked. Any moisture had been leached out of them a while ago. They clung to his tongue like dust. Salty dust.

"The toast got a little burned, but I scraped it off," she said. "You won't even notice, I promise."

Kalila put her fork down as Rafiq spat out the eggs

and started banging on his tray. "He wants his usual, Your Highness," she said by way of explanation.

Isabella's expression fell. "I can get it for him. What does he want?"

"It's okay," Kalila said, hurrying to the pantry and grabbing the baby cereal Rafiq preferred. Within a few moments, she'd set a bowl in front of him and handed him a spoon. Somehow, Kalila found a way to busy herself without returning to her plate.

Adan took another bite while Isabella smiled and fixed her own plate. Then she stood across from him and lifted a forkful of eggs to her mouth. Her frown was immediate.

"I overcooked them," she said, dropping the fork onto the plate and setting it on the counter.

"They're fine," Adan replied. "Just a bit dry."

She reached across the island and gripped his wrist. "Don't, I beg you. If you keep eating, you'll get a stomachache. And then your imperial guard, or whatever you call them, will be marching me off to jail for an attempted assassination."

Adan set his fork on the plate. "You aren't used to this stove," he offered helpfully. "Or the toaster."

She sighed. "Yes, I'm sure that's it. Or maybe I just can't cook as well as I thought I could. I didn't do it that often, actually. I ate takeout quite a lot, in truth."

Adan stood. "Come, let us go out onto the terrace. Kalila will whip something up in no time."

Isabella sighed her disappointment. "Can I help you, Kalila?" she asked.

Kalila shook her head. "Go, Your Highness. This will take me ten minutes. It is very simple. I will be pleased to teach you later, if you like."

"Thank you," Isabella said before following Adan to the terrace. He pulled a chair out for her and she sat heavily.

"I can do nothing right," she said.

Adan grinned as he took the seat across from her. "I don't know about that. I can think of a few things you do exceedingly well."

She didn't seem mollified. "I hate that Kalila has to fix breakfast now. She has enough to do."

"Yes," Adan said, his heart twisting with the familiar grief and love for his old nanny. "This is not too much for her, though. It will be fine."

Her green eyes searched his face then. "You love her, don't you? I thought she was a bit old to be Rafiq's nanny, but then it occurred to me that she must have been yours."

"She is the mother I never had," he replied truthfully, stunning even himself with the admission.

"Your mother died when you were young?"

Adan's laugh wasn't humorous. "Oh, no. She is still very much alive, holding court in her magnificent house, and telling all her friends how proud she is that her son is a king. If she could trot me out for them and pinch my cheeks, she'd be even prouder."

"I'm sorry, Adan," she said softly, frowning.

He shrugged self-consciously. "Her children were prizes. Possessions to be displayed for others to admire. Children made her nervous, so she preferred to see us when we were at our best. And to send us away again once we'd made an impression."

"So Kalila raised you."

"Yes. She was the constant in our lives, the one who held our hands, patched our scrapes and hugged us when we needed it." He sighed. "She should be enjoying her retirement, but there was no one else…."

He broke off when she looked away and pressed a hand to her mouth. When she turned to him again, her eyes were glistening, but she did not cry. Her smile wavered at the corners.

"I did tell you I can't do anything right," she said. "Maybe it would have been better if you hadn't found me after all."

It wasn't so long ago he'd thought that, too, but he wasn't about to say it. He'd been angry for so many things, but he was tired of being angry.

"Why don't we worry about the present, *habibti?* The past cannot be changed."

"Are you truly that forgiving?" she asked, arching an eyebrow. "Or are you just enjoying the fringe benefits?"

In spite of his wish otherwise, a skein of anger began to unwind inside him. And guilt, because he *was* enjoying the sex. Too much, perhaps.

"We've spent one night together, Isabella," he said. "Don't start redecorating everything to your taste just yet."

Isabella didn't know why she'd pushed him. Why hadn't she just gone with the flow and enjoyed breakfast and the sensual afterglow of a night of amazing lovemaking?

Because she was frightened, she admitted to herself. Frightened of what was happening between them, and frightened of her feelings for him and their son. Already, she felt as if leaving would rip her heart from her chest. She'd been attempting, in her own stupid way, to interject reality into the situation.

The reality was that they'd had sex. Mind-blowing sex, but still just sex. One night of pleasure, even if he had been celibate for the past almost three years, was not enough to make him want her to stay forever.

She knew it, but she'd needed to hear it in real terms. She'd needed his censure instead of his warmth so that she could keep her feet firmly grounded. This man was not about to fall in love with her and beg her to stay. He hadn't been in love with her before, so why would he fall now?

If sex were the magic potion, then it would have worked on him years ago. Besides, she was a different person than she had been when they'd married. She didn't need his love. She only needed to be in her son's life. She knew what it was like to grow up without a mother, and she didn't want her son to experience the same. Nor did she want him to be shuffled between parents who used him as a pawn in their relationship.

She would do anything to prevent it.

"I wouldn't dream of redecorating a thing," she said crisply. "I—"

Kalila emerged with a tray just then and Adan shot to his feet to help her. He took the tray from her gnarled hands, admonishing her for not sending one of the serving girls.

"They were busy, Your Excellency," she said. "And it is no problem."

"Adan," he said firmly. "You promised."

The old woman glanced at Isabella, then nodded. "I did. Now be a good husband, Adan, and serve your wife," she said before rambling back into the house.

Isabella bit the inside of her lip as he turned. She wondered if he knew how much emotion showed on his face when he talked to Kalila. She could see it all written there: the love, the guilt, the pain, the frustration.

Her heart throbbed as he came back to her and set the tray down. She wanted to rise to her feet and put her arms around him. To hug him tight and let him know it would all be right. He was a man with so many burdens, and she felt guilty for adding to them.

The food was simple but filling. A copper pot held hot coffee, and Isabella took the handle and poured into two cups. They ate in silence. Isabella looked out over the garden as she chewed. The labyrinth in daylight was a far different place than it had been last night. Less magical, more ordinary.

She thought of their clothes, probably still spread out in the center, and found herself blushing at the memory. Not only that, but a shiver pulsed through her. A pleasurable shiver.

She'd tried not to think too much about what had happened between them—and yet, in truth, she'd hardly thought of anything else. The memories had been playing in the back of her head like a movie reel since she'd awakened this morning. All she could see was Adan's naked body covering hers. All she could feel was the incredible heat and emotion of their lovemaking.

Every stroke of his body into hers had been a revelation. Every kiss, every sigh, every caress. How had she lived each day without knowing that kind of simple joy?

And how had she committed the colossal mistake of allowing last night to happen? It would have been far better had she not. Except that she'd had no will to resist when she'd turned to him in the labyrinth. No will to do anything but see where her feelings took her.

Was that what she'd done two years ago, at her father's house? Followed her feelings to some dark, terrible place that separated her from her baby and her husband? Would she ever know what had truly happened?

"You said that your mother was relieved when you moved out of her house after your recovery," Adan suddenly said, startling her. "Why was that?"

Isabella spread jam on a piece of bread. It had always been hard to think about the many ways in which her relationship with her mother had gone wrong. But perhaps she owed him, since he'd shared his past with her.

"My parents divorced when I was eleven," she said. "I saw my mother rarely after that. My father wouldn't let me go to the States, and my mother wouldn't come to Jahfar. She called frequently at first, but then the calls tapered off. Eventually, she was more like an occasional pen pal than a mother."

"Staying with her was awkward."

"Yes. We were so different by then. I think I appalled her." She chewed the bread. It went down like a lump of sand, flavorless and gritty in her throat.

"Why do you think that?"

"Because she's so independent. And I was too Jahfaran, too traditional. I don't think she liked what my father had made me into." She'd been waiting, in those early days in her mother's house, for someone to tell her what to do. Thinking back on it now, the knowledge filled her with disgust. She'd got over her conditioning, but it hadn't been easy.

"You don't like talking of this," he said.

She shook her head. "I don't, but I probably need to. Maybe I'd remember more if I could face some of the more difficult parts of my life."

His brows drew together. "How do you mean difficult?"

Isabella shrugged. "I was an only child. You know that. And I always felt like such a disappointment to my parents. My father wanted a boy. My mother wanted to please my father. They divorced because of me."

"No one ever divorces because of a child. It's not your fault."

She looked at him in disbelief. "Do they not? Why do you wish to divorce me, then?"

His expression grew fierce. Troubled maybe. "That's different, Isabella."

"But you do intend to divorce me," she insisted. "Nothing has changed in that regard."

He tossed his napkin on the table. "It's a little premature to be discussing our future after only one night, don't you think?"

Isabella's heart throbbed. "You've had a long time to think of your future. I feel like I'm playing catch-up. Like I'm a dog chained to a tree and I can only go so far before the chain snaps me back again."

"What do you want from me, Isabella?" he asked, his eyes flashing in his handsome face. "I'm giving you this time with us. It's all I can promise right now. Because Rafiq comes first, and I will do nothing to compromise his happiness."

Why was she pushing him? Now wasn't the time, and yet she felt so hurt, so lost and alone, that she couldn't seem to help herself. She wanted, just once, for someone to say it would be okay.

And yet she knew that wasn't going to happen. Adan might have enjoyed her body, but he wasn't here to soothe her bruised soul.

The sudden lump in her throat made eating impossible. She pushed her plate away.

"I don't particularly like auditioning for a role in your life, you know." She got to her feet, her hands clenching at her sides. "I didn't come here to do so, either. Because you're right, this *is* about Rafiq. So I'd like to keep the focus where it belongs, if you don't mind."

"And what do you mean by that?" he asked dangerously.

She tilted her chin up. *Courage, Isabella.* "I mean that last night was a mistake I will not be repeating. If you want me in your bed, then you'll have to accept me into your life."

"Are you threatening me, *habibti?*"

She laughed without humor. "As if I could possibly do so. No, I'm telling you that I won't sleep with a man who refuses to give me more than vague promises about my role in my son's life. We don't have to remain together as a couple, Adan, but I *will* be Rafiq's mother until the day I die."

The following week would have been idyllic if not for the tension between her and Adan. He spent a lot of time in his office, on the phone, attending to affairs of state, but he often found time to stop and come to wherever she was sitting and playing with Rafiq. His face remained carefully blank when their eyes met, though when he gazed at Rafiq, the love that showed on his handsome features pierced her heart with its sweetness.

He had not once attempted to touch her or kiss her since her declaration to him.

And she had to admit that she missed the physical contact between them. It had been thrilling, intense and terrifying all at once. She'd thought she would feel more settled, less overwhelmed, if they went back to being strangers to one another.

But nothing could be farther from the truth.

She craved him, craved his heat and scent and passion. One night with him had been the biggest mistake she'd made; because it haunted the rest of her nights and made sleep difficult.

Isabella firmly shoved Adan from her mind as she got dressed and prepared for her day with Rafiq and Kalila. Today, they were going into town to visit the *souq*. It would be their first outing together and she looked forward to it very much.

She met Kalila and Rafiq in the entry, and they walked out to the waiting cars and got inside. Isabella settled Rafiq in his car seat, and then they were rolling toward the small desert town. Rafiq chattered the whole way about things he saw outside the window. Before long, they were in town and Isabella was pushing Rafiq through the *souq* in his stroller. Kalila had said she could do it, but Isabella told her to enjoy the shops instead.

A security detail ranged both behind them and in front of them in order to make sure there were no threats to their safety. It was disconcerting at first, but Isabella soon forgot they were there as she let herself enjoy the outing. The *souq* was colorful, the stalls jammed together haphazardly to create a warren of pathways. There were vendors selling spices, cloth, gold, carpets, copper, clothes and hundreds of other things. Isabella sighed happily. She'd missed this, though she hadn't been allowed to attend the *souq* very often growing up.

Too dangerous, her father had said, when what he really meant was that he didn't have time to take her.

Rafiq stared wide-eyed at the motion and color all around them. Isabella stopped and bought him a honey cake at one of the stalls. She put it on the stroller tray and he dug into the sticky mess with relish.

"His father loved honey cakes at that age, too," Kalila said. "I used to make a special one on his birthday."

Isabella smiled. In the few days she'd spent time with Kalila, the woman had always been so formal and reserved. This was the first time she'd spoken of something personal.

"Was he a handful growing up?" Isabella asked, thinking that he was certainly a handful now.

Kalila laughed. "He was, as you say, a handful," she replied. "But a very loving boy nonetheless. He always regretted starting trouble, though I know he did it for attention."

"His mother's attention?"

Kalila frowned. "And his father's. Mostly his father's, I think. He learned early that his mother was not interested."

"Does he see her often now?"

Kalila shook her head. "Rarely. He ignores her calls. In his own way, I suppose he's paying her back."

Isabella glanced down at Rafiq's dark head. She couldn't imagine her own son feeling that way about her. A wave of love and sadness flooded her. If she had her way, he would never have reason to.

"He is a good man," Kalila continued. "You will need to be patient with him, but he will see what is best."

Isabella drew in a shuddering breath. "I hope you're right, Kalila."

The other woman patted her hand where it rested on the stroller, and they continued their way through the *souq*. The air was hot, and as midmorning approached, it became still and humid.

"We should go back," Isabella decreed after they'd been exploring for nearly an hour. The *abaya* she wore clung to her skin damply, and the headscarf was no longer doing so good a job of keeping the sun out. She'd long ago put up the hood of the stroller so that Rafiq was covered.

She glanced over at Kalila, frowning at her red face. The old woman wore black, which had to be so hot, but she wasn't sweating.

"Yes, we should go," Kalila said.

"Are you feeling well?" Isabella asked as they turned and headed in the direction of the cars.

Kalila waved a hand. Her gait was slow, but steady. "I am fine, Highness."

Isabella handed her a bottle of water from the bag she'd stuffed in the back of the stroller. "Here, drink this."

"You drink it. I can wait."

"No, I insist," Isabella said, twisting off the cap and giving it to Kalila. "Besides, I have more."

It wasn't until ten minutes later, when they were sitting in the car with the cool air blowing, that Kalila cried out. And then she sank in a heap against the seat.

CHAPTER TEN

HEART attack were the only two words he heard when Isabella phoned and said they had taken Kalila to the hospital. Adan ran out the door and hopped into one of the Land Rovers, gunning the engine and speeding out of the driveway before waiting for a driver or security. He made it to the small local hospital in record time, tossing the keys to a startled man in a white coat before dashing into the stark waiting room and demanding to be shown to Kalila's room.

Isabella was sitting on a bench in the hall. She stood as he approached, her face pale and drawn. Anger and fear pierced the veil of his emotions.

"Where is Rafiq?" he demanded before she could speak. First Kalila was ill—and now his son was missing. What was this woman thinking?

Her hands were clasped in front of her body. "There is a playroom nearby. He is there, with a nurse. And he has a bodyguard, never fear."

Guilt rippled through him, but he could not voice it. Instead, he turned to the door of Kalila's room.

"Before you go in—" Isabella said behind him.

He turned, one eyebrow lifted in question.

"The doctor is with her, but he won't tell you this in

front of her. She can't work anymore, Adan. She can't take care of Rafiq. Her heart is weak. She's on medication, but it can't make up for her advancing age."

"And that suits you just fine, doesn't it?" he snapped. "If you think this is your lucky opportunity, Isabella, think again."

She looked as if he'd slapped her. The guilt washing through him turned into a wave.

"I'll forgive you for that because I know how much you love her," she said quietly. "You're scared and hitting out at me. I understand that. But don't you dare think I would ever take joy in someone else's pain. That's not fair."

He ground his teeth together.

"You're right," he said. And then he turned and entered Kalila's room.

After another two hours, Isabella took Rafiq home. It was time for his dinner and there was nothing more they could do at the hospital. Kalila was in a private room, receiving the best care money could buy, and Adan was with her. She was weak and tired, but the doctors seemed to think she would recover.

She just wouldn't be allowed to take care of growing boys anymore. She needed rest, relaxation and someone to take care of her for a change. Her husband had died several years ago, and she had no children of her own. She'd been living with her sister's family when Adan brought her back to the palace to care for Rafiq, and Isabella supposed that was where she would return.

It made her sad to think of Kalila leaving her son. Rafiq was attached to her, and no matter what Adan had said, Isabella did not rejoice in the fact that Rafiq's care would fall to her with Kalila gone. She wanted to be a mother to her boy, but not at anyone's expense.

Worse, she felt as if Kalila's attack had been her fault. If she hadn't wanted to go to the *souq,* if Kalila hadn't insisted on walking with her—if, if, *if...*

There were too many ifs, and she knew it wasn't right to blame herself. The doctor had told her that Kalila's heart was weak and an attack had been inevitable.

Still...

Isabella shook herself from her reverie. She had the cook prepare dinner for her and Rafiq, then took her son to his room and let him play for a little while before bathing him and putting him to bed. He was fussy, missing Kalila, but she stood over his crib and sang until he began to drift. Once he was asleep, she bent and gave him a kiss, then retreated to her own room, taking the monitor that Kalila relied upon to tell her if Rafiq was awake.

The sun was just setting when she heard a car pull up outside. Doors slammed and then slammed again as Adan entered the palace. She waited a few minutes before going in search of him. He'd been gone so long, and she was worried that maybe something had changed with Kalila's condition.

She found him in his office, sitting in the darkening room and gazing out the window. His computer wasn't on, so she knew he wasn't working.

"Adan? Is everything all right?"

He didn't turn. "She will recover," he said. "But she's very tired tonight."

"Yes, I imagine she would be." Isabella bit her lip. "Do you need anything?"

He sighed and shoved a hand through his hair. "It's my fault," he said. "All my fault."

Isabella's heart cracked in two. "Adan, no." She went to him and put a hand on his shoulder. Squeezed. "It's not your fault. It's no one's fault." She swallowed a raft of tears. "And if you want to play the blame game, I'll say that I think it's *my* fault. I took her to the *souq*, and I kept her out in the heat too long..."

A sob welled in her chest and she stuffed her fist against her mouth to keep it from coming out. This was about him, not her. About his feelings and fears, not about her insecurities. Damn her, why couldn't she just comfort him and not make it about *her* for once?

Adan turned the chair and wrapped his arms around her waist, stunning her with the motion. He buried his head against her chest, his breathing coming faster and harder now, as if he, too, was working not to lose control. A tremor slid from his body to hers, and she put her arms around him and squeezed tight.

She didn't know how long they stayed that way, but the light in the sky had died away completely when his grip finally eased. She couldn't stop herself from cupping his jaw, from bending and pressing her lips to his forehead.

His hands slid to her buttocks, and a thrill of anticipation snapped over her nerve endings. She threaded her fingers in his hair, lowered her lips to his and drank him in.

They didn't speak because words weren't needed. They each knew what the other wanted. What they needed.

He undressed her with quick hands while she did the same for him. Soon, they were naked and pressed together, their skin hot, their hands seeking, their sighs and moans and kisses only the beginning. He set her on the desk and stepped between her legs. Then he was deep inside her and they were both gasping and groaning with the incredible sensation. Papers fell to the floor as he took her hard, but he didn't seem to care.

Isabella wrapped her legs tightly around his waist, lifted herself to him, and let her head fall back as he took her body to heights she'd been dreaming of for the past week.

It was so good. So right.

Tears slipped down her cheeks unchecked. She was glad it was so dark, because she was afraid of what he would think if he saw her crying. Would he know she cried because he'd ripped her heart out of her chest and claimed it for his own? Would he know that, in spite of herself, she'd managed to fall for him? That she saw through him, through the facade of the harsh desert lord to the soft, inner core of the man who loved his old nanny so much he would shed silent tears for her?

She cried for herself, too. For the naive, stupid girl she must have been. And for the woman she was now—the woman who would have her heart shattered if this man decided to let her go at the end of their two weeks.

She'd come to Jahfar to find out the truth. She'd found something much more precious.

She didn't know what had happened between them two years ago, or why she'd walked into the desert and been lost, but she knew that *right now,* she loved this man. She loved him and their child so much she would do anything for them.

Soon, she forgot her tears as her body wound so tight that she knew she was about to explode.

"Yes, Adan, oh yes," she gasped as he lifted her hips from the desk and ground into her, forcing her into a shattering orgasm that caused black spots to appear behind her eyes. He continued to drive into her—and then his release hit him and he groaned her name as his body stiffened and shuddered.

A few moments later, he gathered her to him and kissed her softly. They held each other for several minutes, not speaking, just breathing.

"Spend the night with me," he whispered in her ear.

A shiver skated down her spine. "Yes," she said simply.

Isabella was awakened in the night by Rafiq's cries. She stumbled from the bed where Adan was sleeping so soundly, the covers shoved down to reveal his naked body in all its magnificence. He lay on his back, one leg bent, an arm thrown casually over his head.

He stirred as she moved, then came awake as if a switch had been thrown inside him.

"Where are you going, *habibti?*" he asked.

"Rafiq," she whispered, holding up the monitor. "He's crying."

She went into the nursery and found her son standing in his crib. It took her a while to figure out that he had a messy diaper, but she managed to change it without too much trouble. Then she sang him to sleep again. When she turned to leave, Adan was standing in the door, watching her. He'd pulled on a pair of shorts, but his chest was bare, gleaming in the tiny night-light illuminating the room. His hair was mussed, and he shoved a hand through it, yawning.

"He's sleeping," Isabella whispered as she came over to him.

"You did a good job with him," Adan whispered back. "He's comfortable with you."

She felt ridiculously pleased at that. "I'm learning. But he's very patient with me."

Adan smiled. "Patient? I'd never have called our son patient. He's too much like me."

Isabella didn't miss his use of the plural. Hope blossomed in her soul. *Careful, Isabella. It doesn't mean anything, except that he's tired and stressed.*

He put his arm around her and they walked back to his room in silence. Once there, he stripped the robe from her body and kissed his way across her skin, taking his time, until she was writhing on the bed and aching for his possession.

He made love to her again, tenderly, drawing out the pleasure between them until there was nothing else that existed in this world but the two of them. Isabella came apart beneath him, and then slowly pieced herself back together.

Melancholy set in as they lay together afterward. She was no closer to remembering her life with him than she ever had been. She'd remembered pieces, but not the whole. And she hadn't yet remembered a thing about her baby.

She didn't want this time together to end, but she also wanted to see her father. She had to know what had happened and why he'd lied about it to her. Part of her worried that it was something horrible. Something devastating from which she would never recover if she knew the truth.

And part of her *had* to know the truth if she was to

move forward and build a life with Adan and her son. Adan hadn't said anything, but the way he touched her, the way he made love to her and held her—surely he'd decided they would stay together and parent their son as a couple?

He could not be so cruel as to give her false hope, could he? If he truly intended to send her away, would he have asked her to sleep with him tonight? It had not been about sex at that moment. They'd gone to his bed and fallen asleep in each other's arms until Rafiq's cries awoke them.

Now, Adan's fingers were stroking up and down her arm. Softly, rhythmically.

"I'm sorry for what I said to you earlier. About Kalila." His voice startled her, and she turned on her side to face him, spread her hand over his chest and delighted in the feel of smooth hot skin and hard muscle. A sensual shiver slid across her. She wasn't interested in sex right now, but touching him made her body stretch and come to life in places that should be too sated to do so.

"I know, Adan. You were scared for her. We both were."

"I shouldn't have brought her out of retirement," he said. "But there was no one else I trusted."

Isabella sighed wistfully. "She wouldn't have come had she not wanted to."

"Yes, but I shouldn't have asked. I should have searched harder for someone else. I should have married sooner."

Isabella felt a pinprick of anxiety. But what else could he say? He hadn't known she was alive then, she reminded herself. "You probably should have," she said. "And yet I'm glad you did not."

He turned his head on the pillow. "You have complicated my life, *habibti*, but I find I am not sorry for it. You love Rafiq very much, and this makes me happy."

I love you very much, too, she wanted to say. But she didn't. It was too soon, too fresh, and she was still frightened of it. Frightened of how vulnerable it made her. When she'd been alone in Hawaii, she'd known something was missing from her life. But she hadn't known what that was. Now that she did, the thought of losing it again terrified her.

And if she didn't quite know how she'd lost it the first time, how could she prevent it happening a second time?

"He's amazing," she said. "I can't believe we made him together. It astounds me every time I look at him. He has so much of you in him, and yet I see me, too."

"I must find another nanny for him," Adan said on a sigh.

Her stomach flipped, but then she told herself not to read too much into it. A nanny was not unusual in the least, especially for the son of a king.

"Can Kalila recommend someone?" she asked.

He nodded slowly. "I had not thought of it before, but yes, I will ask her once she's feeling better."

"How will you break it to her that she can no longer care for him?"

She could see the gleam of his teeth as he smiled in the darkness. "Kalila would never refuse an order from her king. I plan to buy her a house in Port Jahfar, on the coast, and fill it with servants to take care of her. I should have done this in the first place, but I admit I did not think of it. I was a teen when she left my parents' employ, and though I saw her from time to time, it wasn't frequent enough that I wondered what she was doing in her retirement."

Her heart squeezed. "You are very good to her, Adan. She's lucky to have you."

"No," he said. "It is I who am lucky to have her. And I want her to know it for as long as she lives. Between me and my siblings, she will never want for company. We will visit her often, and I will bring her to the palace as frequently as she desires, provided her doctor approves."

"I'm so glad she's going to be all right," Isabella said, shivering as she remembered the way Kalila had collapsed on the seat. Her eyes had rolled back in her head, and Isabella had thought she was dead.

He squeezed her hand where it lay on his chest. "You aren't to blame, you know. The doctor said it was lucky someone was with her when it happened. If she'd been in her bed, she would have died before we found her. The heat in the *souq* exacerbated her condition, but it did not cause it."

Isabella shivered again. "Then I'm glad it happened the way it did, even if she frightened me half to death. I was certain that if anything happened to her, you would never forgive me. Nor would I forgive myself," she admitted. "Kalila has been kind to me. She's never once made me feel as if I don't belong."

"Maybe it's because you do," he said softly.

They stayed at the Butterfly Palace for two more days before packing everything up and returning to Port Jahfar. Though the trip had been cut short, Adan felt as if he'd learned all he needed to know. Now he had to get back to the capital and continue the process of governing his nation.

Kalila was being airlifted to the finest hospital in Port Jahfar, where she would continue to receive care from the best heart specialist in the country.

Adan worked on his laptop and took calls while they traveled, but he hadn't been able to take a separate vehicle from Isabella and Rafiq. He should have, perhaps, but he hadn't wanted to.

His gaze kept straying to his wife. She was beautiful, radiant and so much more confident and self-aware than he'd ever given her credit for in the past. He'd said she was a different person, and perhaps in some ways she was, but this luminous woman had always been there.

He just hadn't been able to see her.

She looked up from where she sat playing a simple game with Rafiq and caught his eye. Then she smiled at him, that lovely, secretive smile that sent blood pooling low in his groin. Always, he wanted her. This feeling hadn't abated since he'd taken her in the labyrinth over a week ago.

If anything, it had grown stronger.

This morning, they'd made frantic love against the marble-tiled wall of the shower, him holding her up and thrusting into her tight, wet body while she clasped him around the waist and rode him with abandon. Last night, he'd taken her from behind as she knelt on all fours in the center of the bed. He'd wrapped his hands in her glorious hair and lost himself in the heat and wonder of her.

And still he wanted more. Had he wanted her this much when they'd married? He didn't remember it being so overwhelming, this compulsion. He did remember enjoying her body very much, though he hadn't enjoyed her in quite so many earthy and raw ways.

She was his match in bed. His equal. And he was beginning to believe she was his equal outside of it, as well. She wasn't Jasmine Shadi. She wasn't quiet or meek or easily cowed. She wouldn't agree with him on everything. And she wouldn't tell him what he wanted to hear just to keep peace between them.

Adan frowned. He still didn't know why she'd left, why she'd abandoned her baby son, and that bothered him a great deal. If he kept her, was he endangering Rafiq's happiness? Was she only playing the good mother now because she wanted to be a queen? At the first sign of trouble, would she hand Rafiq off to a nanny and claim that he was too much for her nerves?

No. To the depths of his soul, he knew the answer to that question. Isabella was not like his mother. She would not ignore her child. His mother couldn't have faked deep love for her children for any amount of money. She'd loved them in her own way, but her way was twisted to suit her own purposes. They were a means to an end, a possession to be proud of. They weren't meant to be hugged and kissed and loved.

Isabella wasn't like that. He'd watched her changing Rafiq's diaper when she hadn't known he was there. Other than not quite knowing what to do, she hadn't acted like a woman who would rather be anywhere but where she was. She loved Rafiq. He couldn't be more certain of it if it were written in indelible ink across her forehead.

She *loved* their child. And he found he didn't mind so

much sharing Rafiq with her after all. It seemed natural to do so.

Still, he spent the journey weighing the pros and cons. By the time they reached Port Jahfar, Adan knew what he was going to do. There was only one decision he could make. One decision that was right for them all.

He stepped from the car, and Mahmoud, who had returned earlier in the day, bowed deeply. "Your Excellency. Welcome home."

"Thank you, Mahmoud."

Around them, servants hurried forward to gather luggage while his security team fanned out to oversee the procedure.

Mahmoud shot a glance at Isabella. Then he gave Adan a meaningful look.

"There is a *gentleman* here to see you, Excellency. A gentleman you have been desiring to see since your return from America."

CHAPTER ELEVEN

ISABELLA had just put Rafiq down for his afternoon nap. She closed the door to his room and settled into the living area that connected Rafiq's nursery to Adan's suite. A television flashed silent pictures on the screen. She didn't bother to pick up the remote and turn on the sound. Instead, she opened up a laptop computer that was sitting on a side table and surfed the web. She hadn't been on a computer since she'd arrived in Jahfar nearly two weeks ago. Her email was overrun, but she set about methodically answering her friends back on Maui.

The band wanted to know when she was coming back. They'd hired a temporary singer, but they needed her dreadfully. She laughed at the number of exclamation points that Kurt, the guitarist, put in his email.

A knock sounded on the door. She waited, expecting a servant to enter, but when no one did, she got up and opened it.

"Daddy?"

"Isabella," he said, his plump face creased in a frown. There was sorrow on that face. And fear. But fear for what? For her?

Her heart pounded with worry—and just as quickly, the worry changed to anger. He'd lied to her. Whatever had happened to her, he'd *lied*. She stepped back to let him in, folding her arms around her like a shield.

"Does Adan know you're here?"

"I have just been to see him," he said, taking a handkerchief from his pocket and mopping the sheen of sweat that glistened on his brow.

"And did you tell him what he wanted to know?" she asked, proud of how her voice didn't betray her cold fury.

"I told him enough."

"Then perhaps you can tell me what the hell really happened to me," she said very precisely, the words like razor blades in her throat.

He looked at her in surprise. She expected a sharp correction any second, but he did nothing of the sort. Good, because she would never be meek and dutiful ever again.

"I wanted to protect you," he said. "I did it to protect you."

"Protect me from what? And don't you dare lie to me now, not after what I've been through."

He took out a cheroot and lit it with shaking hands. She moved away, not caring for the smoke, yet realizing he needed it to calm down. Adan must have taken him to task for his deception. The thought satisfied her immensely.

"You were sick, Isabella," he said when he'd drawn in a lungful of smoke and let it out again. "You weren't yourself after the baby came."

A chill skated over her. She spun to face him. "Not myself? How do you mean?"

"You were depressed. Postnatal depression, the doctor

said. You were distant, uninvolved with the baby. And you talked of suicide."

"I don't believe you," she whispered past the huge lump in her throat. How could that be possible?

His face twisted. "Believe it, Isabella. Do you think I went through what I did for you just because it seemed like a fun idea?"

She swallowed. Hard. "Adan's never said anything to me about being depressed. Why not? Wouldn't he have known?"

"He didn't know because I didn't want him to know," her father snapped. "I couldn't afford for him to know. He would have had you declared insane, Isabella. And then he would have divorced you."

Fear wrapped around her heart and squeezed. Insane? Would Adan have done that? She shook her head. No, he would have helped her, not hurt her. He would have wanted her to get well.

"So you believed it was better he thought I was dead?" Anger—and fear—was a living thing inside her belly, twisting and turning and lashing her with its claws.

"It was better for everyone."

Horror permeated her bones as she stared at him. How could he have done it? How could he have been more concerned about his station and his business interests than about her?

Because she knew what had motivated him as surely as if he'd blazoned it across the sky. *I couldn't afford for him to know...*

If a prince had divorced his daughter for being suicidal and depressed, then he would lose respect. His business would suffer.

Prince Weds Daughter of Prominent Businessman

would have become Prince Divorces Insane Daughter
of Prominent Businessman.

"How did you do it? How did you make everyone
think I'd died?" she said, her lip trembling. She needed
to hear it. Needed to hear to what lengths her father had
gone to "protect" her.

To protect himself. Because, once more, she'd managed to disappoint him, hadn't she? He'd wed her to a
prince, and she'd ruined everything.

He finished the cheroot and stubbed it out. "You
really did walk into the desert, Isabella. We couldn't
find you. It was two weeks before I got word that a
woman resembling you had been taken to a hospital in
Oman. You were found by British tourists who kept you
alive long enough to get you there."

Her eyes were flooding with tears. "Why can't I remember any of this?"

"Because you were near death, because you blocked
it from your mind—I don't know! When I realized you
didn't know you had a child or a husband, I had you
examined by a psychiatrist. He said you were repressing
memories that were painful to you."

Painful memories? About Adan and Rafiq?

"But why didn't you tell Adan? I might have remembered if he'd come for me. I'd have been with my baby
for these past two years instead of living somewhere
else and believing the lies you told me."

He shook his head. "You would not have magically
remembered, Isabella. And Adan wouldn't have let you
near Rafiq once he realized you were so unstable."

He came over to her, put his hands on her shoulders.
She wanted to shrug away from him, but she was too
numb to do so.

"I know you don't believe this, but I did what I thought was best for you. You're my only child, and I love you. I would have sooner had you living somewhere else and not knowing about your past than to have you committed to an institution. It was a blessing that you had forgotten."

"You don't know that he would have done that."

"He is an Al Dhakir, Isabella, and he bears a great responsibility. More so now than before. He could not have afforded the attention. He most definitely cannot do so now."

A chill skated over her. "What do you mean by that? It's over. I'm back, and though I don't remember, I'm fine."

"For now," he said, his eyes full of sadness as he gazed at her. "But what if you were to get pregnant again?"

She shook him off. "I don't remember any of what you're saying. I can't just believe what you tell me when I don't know the truth!"

"I'm telling you the truth, child. You were depressed once—it's possible you could be so again. And who knows what you will do next time?"

She swiped at her eyes with trembling hands. "They make medication for depression. It won't happen again."

"You were on medication the last time, though I made sure your husband didn't know about it. But you didn't take it, Isabella, and look what happened. Do you want to take that chance again? Do you want to embarrass your husband, your nation, by trying to harm yourself or your baby? What if you succeed the next time? What then?"

She wanted to put her hands over her ears, like a recalcitrant child, and shut him out. She wanted to lock out the painful words and pretend she'd never heard them. How could she have done such a thing? What was *wrong* with her? Why couldn't she be normal, like any other woman who'd just had a baby?

Why wasn't she normal?

"What are you suggesting I do?" she asked. Part of her was gibbering in fear and the other part, the rational part, had locked on to cool, disconnected control. The only way to get through this was to not feel anything.

He sank onto one of the couches and steepled his hands beneath his chin. "Go back to the States, Isabella. Go back and forget any of this happened."

Tears dropped down her cheeks though she tried not to let them. "I can't do that," she said. "I won't do it. I'm not leaving my baby ever again."

He sighed and got to his feet once more. "You may not have a choice. Adan knows everything now. And he may not be willing to give you another chance."

She waited hours for Adan to come. The sun passed high overhead, then slowly sank into the sea, and still he did not come. He had to come eventually, because she was still in his apartments and Rafiq was still with her. She sat on the couch in the living area, a home-improvement program on the television while Rafiq played with a set of building blocks on the floor.

The people on television were so happy, fixing up their modest home with new curtains, paint and furniture. Newlyweds with a baby on the way, the host helpfully informed her.

Isabella splayed her fingers across her stomach. Had

she ever been that happy? Had she made plans with her husband for their home and their new baby, or had she simply done what she'd been told and not asked questions or dared to have an opinion?

She was very afraid she knew the correct answer.

Was that why she'd forgotten everything? Had she been so miserable that she simply couldn't face it? Was she that *weak* that she couldn't face her own past?

Angrily, she tossed the remote onto the couch. She was so wound up she wanted to punch something. She would have hauled off and socked the cushion off the couch, but it would make a noise and Rafiq would jump since he was so engrossed in his play. And she didn't want to frighten him. He was her precious, precious child. Her chest hurt with all the love she felt for him. How could she have ever dreamed of harming him?

Stop. She couldn't go there. She simply couldn't think it. Besides, she didn't know if it was even remotely true. She'd tried to harm herself, not him. She might not remember what had happened then, but she knew in her bones she could never harm her child.

Another hour passed and she put Rafiq to bed, then returned to the living area. She couldn't go to the rooms she'd been given when she'd arrived, because that would mean leaving Rafiq alone. And she couldn't go and lie down in Adan's bed since she was no longer certain he would want her there.

She fell asleep on the couch finally, curled up in a ball with the remote in her fist. When she woke again, the only light in the room was the glow of the television. She pushed herself up, yawning—

And squeaked as she realized she wasn't alone.

Adan sat in a chair across from her. He was watching

her, waiting—for what? For her to go crazy before his eyes?

She wouldn't give him the satisfaction.

"You talked to my father, I take it," she said. What sense in delaying the inevitable?

"I did."

"And so now you know."

"How are you, Isabella?"

The question made her angry. As if he was now worried about her sanity and needed to treat her with kid gloves. "Other than wanting to clap tinfoil on my head to keep the aliens from finding me, I feel just fine," she retorted.

He didn't crack a smile. "Did anything he said jog your memory?"

She crossed her arms. "No. I walked into the desert and nearly died. People found me. I woke up with a big gaping hole in my memory where you and Rafiq should have been. End of story."

She suddenly deflated, pulling her knees up to her chest and wrapping her arms around them. "It's frightening not to remember what happened to you, especially when people tell you things you said or did and you just don't remember any of it. It's like it happened to someone else, or maybe it's just a movie someone tells you about. Because it can't be you. If it were, you would remember."

He turned his head toward the closed door to Rafiq's room. "How has he been today, without Kalila?"

She shoved a stray lock of hair behind her ear. He didn't want to talk about it, of course. The moment they got to the difficult parts, he was done. Could she blame him? It was creepy, in a way.

"He fussed a bit, but he's been fine. He asks where she is. I told him she was sick and she had to go away to feel better."

"Do you think that's wise?"

"Yes," she said firmly. "He can't understand the full truth, but he doesn't need to be lied to, either. When I was five, my dog died. My parents couldn't tell me the truth—" Here she paused and shook her head. "Oh God, of course they couldn't." A bitter laugh erupted from her throat before she stuffed it down again. "They told me he ran away. For years I kept hoping he would come home again, wondering if I'd done something wrong to make him leave. It was harder when I learned what really happened, years after the fact."

He was looking at her with sympathy. She almost hated it, almost hated the way he seemed to see her as a fragile creature when only a few hours before he'd treated her like an equal. She didn't delude herself that he'd fallen in love with her, but she'd thought he was beginning to care. How could he ever care about someone as broken as she was? He'd always be wondering when she was going to crack again.

"Then I guess you were right to tell him."

"What happens now, Adan?" she asked. Because she just didn't feel like beating around the bush.

He stood. "It's late. We should probably go to bed."

Disappointment ate at her. She *was* tired, but she'd hoped he would say more. That he would tell her he'd been thinking about what came next. That he would say something about what her father had said, other than to ask if she was all right. She wanted to know how *he* felt about it.

But he wasn't going to tell her. Not tonight anyway.

"I had you moved closer," he said. "Your room is across from Rafiq's now."

Her room. He didn't even want to sleep with her anymore.

"Great," she said. Because what else was she going to say?

He walked over to a door and opened it for her. "Get some sleep, Isabella. We'll talk in the morning."

She paused in the doorway. Her hands itched to reach out to him. She wanted to wrap her arms around him, wanted him to wrap his around her and squeeze her tight. She wanted comfort and connection.

But he wanted away from her. Away from his crazy wife. Her heart hurt.

She wrapped her arms around herself to keep from touching him.

"Good night, Adan," she said. And then she went inside and closed the door.

Adan lay in his big, lonely bed and longed for Isabella. She'd seemed so tired, so fragile and worn-out, and he'd known he couldn't ask anything of her. He'd thought of taking her to his bed and just holding her, but he hadn't trusted himself to keep from doing anything else once he had her in his arms.

She'd had a lot to process this afternoon.

So had he.

He was still so angry with Hassan Maro that the man was lucky he wasn't sitting in the bottom of Port Jahfar's darkest prison cell at the moment. After he'd spoken with Maro, he'd gained access to the rest of Isabella's medical records. The doctor he'd had talk to her upon their arrival had examined everything and called him back immediately, confirming the findings.

Isabella had been suffering from postnatal depression, as he'd earlier thought, and she'd nearly died in the desert. Further, she'd chosen to block certain memories of her life as a coping mechanism for the emotions that had driven her out there in the first place.

Adan turned over and punched the pillow, his body aching. But his heart ached more. He'd thought back to the early days of their marriage and tried to remember what had happened between them. Not much, he had to admit. He'd taken her virginity, got her pregnant and left her to her own devices while he ran his businesses and waited for the birth of their child.

They had not been close.

She'd bored him, mostly. She'd done everything she was supposed to do as his wife, but she hadn't challenged him or made him long to come home at the end of the day. She hadn't even sung for him—and singing was such a part of her that she was constantly singing or humming something. How had he never realized that before?

Oddly enough, as much as she'd angered him when he'd found her again, she'd also electrified him. She'd made his blood hum with anticipation, and she hadn't stopped since the moment he'd kissed her in the back room of that seedy little bar in Hawaii.

Guilt was his constant companion now. Was it his fault she'd been so miserable two years ago? Why hadn't he paid her closer attention after Rafiq's birth? Why hadn't he known she was suffering?

Damn Hassan Maro for hiding it from him!

Had he caused her to feel so hopeless that she'd tried

to take her own life? The doctor had said it had nothing to do with him and everything to do with the hormones raging through her body, but why had she blocked her memories of him specifically?

He couldn't figure it out. And he knew he wouldn't figure it out even if he lay here for an entire month of sleepless nights. He would simply go round and round with feelings of guilt and anger and helplessness.

What he had to think about now was the future. Their future. He sighed heavily. Nothing was as he'd planned it.

He'd wanted to marry Jasmine because she was a friend, and because she was kind and gentle and would be a good mother to Rafiq and any other children they had.

But he couldn't do it. As he'd lain in bed with Isabella the night of Kalila's attack, he'd known the truth.

He couldn't take another woman to his bed, couldn't make love to her, when all he would be able to think about was Isabella. Somewhere over the past few days, Isabella had become vital to him. She made his blood sing, his heart pound and his body ache.

But it was more than that. She was so vibrant to him, so alive and beautiful, and she loved their son completely. He couldn't imagine his life without her in it.

Was that love? He didn't know, but he knew he wanted to find out. When he looked at Rafiq, he was overwhelmed with love—but it was different than what he felt when he looked at Isabella. What he felt for her was strong, but was it based on attraction or on something deeper?

He wasn't sure. How could he be sure?

And now, on top of everything else, he was worried about her. Could he give her what she needed, or were they doomed to repeat this cycle again? Could he make her happy, or was he incapable of doing so?

He wanted to fix it, wanted to make everything right again, and yet he did not know how.

He was a king, with a nation to lead and people to govern, and he couldn't even figure out his personal life. What did that say about him?

CHAPTER TWELVE

SOMETHING had changed between them. Isabella concentrated on the breakfast they'd been served beneath the Moorish arches of the inner courtyard, which adjoined the royal apartments. The food tasted like ash on her tongue.

She tried to read the same article in *Al-Arab Jahfar* for the twentieth time that morning, and for the twentieth time she couldn't get past the first paragraph without her mind wandering.

Adan sat across from her, his attention firmly on the folder of papers that Mahmoud had brought to him as they'd sat down to eat. He'd barely spoken to her since.

Not that she was surprised. He was horrified, no doubt, by what her father had told him. And he was merely tolerating her until he could find someone he trusted to replace Kalila. Or until he could divorce her and marry the woman he'd been planning to wed when he'd found her in Hawaii.

The thought made her stomach cramp. How could he have made love to her so passionately only yesterday morning if he'd still been planning to marry someone else? Not only that, but what about the things they'd shared with each other? It hadn't been just about sex, she was certain.

For her, it was about love. Her heart hurt with all the love she felt for him. Had it been this way before? Was she getting a taste of what it had felt like to be with him before she'd walked into the desert? She very much feared she was. Not only that, but she was also getting a taste of what it was like to be the only one whose heart was on the line.

Last night, she'd asked him what happened next. She'd been tired and heartbroken and she'd wanted to know. Now, she was too scared to repeat the question.

He'd given her a reprieve last night. He'd pitied her, no doubt, and he'd wanted to spare her feelings.

But today? Today he would tell her the bald truth. And she just wasn't ready to hear it.

Later, she would face facts, but for now she wanted to pretend everything was as it had been before. She wanted a few hours to remember what it had been like before her father had interjected the ugly truth of what had really happened to her.

She wanted to remember that she'd been building something precious with Adan and her son. Something she might never get back again.

"I am going to visit Kalila this morning," Adan said, startling her with the sound of his voice after so much silence. "I will ask her for recommendations about a nanny."

Isabella hooked her finger into her coffee cup, willing it not to tremble.

And so it began.

"That's probably a good idea," she said. "It will take time to find someone good."

"Yes," he said. "There is much to do in the coming weeks. It would be nice to have a new nanny in place to make everything go as smoothly as possible."

Isabella was proud of herself that she took a sip of her coffee without spilling any. "You're right. The sooner, the better."

She thought he looked at her oddly, but it was gone so fast she wasn't certain.

"What do you intend to do today, Isabella?" he asked. Clearly, he wanted to move on to small talk now that they'd gotten that out of the way.

She shrugged. "I was thinking of taking Rafiq to the pool."

"That's good," Adan said. "Rafiq loves to swim."

"And what about you?" she asked. "What will you do after you visit Kalila?"

His fingers drummed on the folder he'd laid on the table. He was so distant now, so polite, and it frustrated her. Where was the man who'd held her close in the night? The man who'd shared his darkest secrets with her?

"I have many things to attend to," he said. He looked at her then, his dark eyes piercing to her soul. "I don't know when I'll be done this evening."

Her heart sank a little. "So we should eat without you?"

He inclined his head. That dark, handsome head she wanted to cup between her hands while her fingers combed through his crisp curls.

"It would probably be best. In fact," he said, rising, "I should go now or I will never get through the day's tasks."

Isabella waited, for what she didn't know. Their eyes

met for a long minute, and her pulse kicked up higher and higher with each passing second. *Say something, Adan. Say you missed me last night. Say you want me tonight. Say it.*

But he didn't say anything. He simply turned and walked away.

Isabella took Rafiq to the kiddie pool where he splashed and played while she sat on the edge and watched him. The pool was partially shaded, but the weather was hot and she didn't drink enough water, even though someone continually brought her a fresh glass whenever the ice melted. She knew she was spending too much time fretting about the past, the future—and the present—but she couldn't seem to stop.

Two weeks ago, before Adan had crashed into her life again, she'd been happy enough—if a bit lonely and empty. She'd thought it was simply melancholy.

Today she had so much more to lose—and it terrified her. Which, in turn, made her angry. Since when had she reverted to the man-pleasing mind-set she'd grown up with? What did it matter if he didn't want her? She didn't have to let it control her life. Not everyone was lucky in love, after all.

People had their hearts broken all the time. People survived. She would, too.

When Rafiq started to get fussy, she took him back to his room and put him down for a nap. By then she had a headache, so she took some of the migraine medicine that Adan had got for her, closed the shutters to keep out the sun and lay on the bed in the darkened room, hoping the headache would soon abate.

She drifted in and out of sleep, her mind working on

so many things that at first she didn't quite realize what the scenes and emotions trickling into her head were. It began as a memory here or there, a snippet of life, until finally she sat bolt upright with a gasp.

Her heart thundered in her ears: she'd remembered her life with Adan.

They weren't the kind of memories where everything suddenly returned with such clarity and force that she could point to a moment in time and say, "This is when it happened. This is what caused it."

Instead, it was a body of knowledge downloaded into her head almost randomly, but nonetheless completely— or as completely as it would ever be. It was the emotion that slammed into her first, the helpless knowledge of what it was like to be in love with a man who did not love you. Or, worse, respect you.

Humiliation beat down on her. She'd tried everything to be a good wife to him. But after he'd got her pregnant, he'd become uninterested. Politely uninterested, just like this morning. She'd rearranged everything for him, suppressed her likes and dislikes to make sure he was comfortable and happy.

They took meals together often at first, and then rarely. He stopped coming to her bed. He did not make it to doctor's appointments, and he was often out of town.

She recalled growing big with child, recalled the sickness—the never-ending sickness that even now caused a pang of nausea to roll through her in sympathy—and her terror when the time came to give birth.

Adan had not been there. No one had been there, except for a servant. Her father was out of the country, and of course her mother was in America. Adan's mother was a stranger, a woman she'd met at the wedding and a handful of times since, who'd struck her as a cold, self-centered woman. She'd met his brothers, and his sister, but they were strangers to her, as well.

She'd given birth in a sterile hospital room, her closest friend the obstetrician who'd seen her through the pregnancy.

A drop of water splashed onto her breast, surprising her. She ran a hand across her cheeks, realized she was crying.

Of course she was crying. The memories were desolate, lonely. It's no wonder she had forgotten.

She ran through Rafiq's birth, remembering the agony of the contractions, the relief of the epidural and the moment when they'd handed her her child. She remembered feeling numb. She hadn't known what to do, and she'd only wanted to cry when someone insisted she put the baby to her breast. She'd wanted to escape. She remembered that clearly.

Shame and guilt hammered into her. She remembered feeling so strange, so disconnected, and she remembered not wanting to hold her baby. She remembered resenting Rafiq for imprisoning her in a routine that required her to subordinate even more of her self than she already had. Yet another male demanding that she change for him, that she be the perfect ideal of what a wife and mother should be.

Sorrow pounded through her in waves.

Oh God, she was every bit as horrible as Adan had thought she was. She hadn't wanted her baby. She'd wanted to escape, to be someone else.

She'd certainly tried to escape, hadn't she? For a time, she'd succeeded.

Except that she'd given up the one thing that was the most important thing in the world to her: her son. She'd asked herself for the past two weeks how she could have done such a thing. Now she knew, and the knowledge crushed her soul.

Isabella buried her face in the pillow and cried. She screamed and punched the pillow and kicked the bed until she was spent, until she had no energy left. She was a terrible person. She was damaged and sick, and she didn't deserve to be forgiven for anything.

She allowed herself to lie there wallowing in self-pity until the moment she heard a tiny cry on the monitor. Then she swung herself from the bed, sniffling, and took a deep breath to calm herself.

Whatever had happened in the past, she was Rafiq's mother now. She loved him. She would do anything for him, including sacrifice her happiness for his. She would never be that helpless, sad creature she'd been two years ago ever again.

She went and got Rafiq from his crib, then combed her hair and fixed her face before changing into a dress and a pair of low heels. She wanted to see Adan, wanted to tell him that she'd remembered. She didn't know why it was important, but it seemed as if she should tell him.

She picked Rafiq up, remembering to grab his favorite toy bear. A servant told her where to find the administrative wing as she left the royal apartments. She hummed to Rafiq on the way. He twisted a lock of her hair around his fingers, his bear clutched in the other hand.

Thinking of everything she'd remembered about his birth and the aftermath, she squeezed him a little too tightly. He started to fuss so she eased her grip again and smiled as she sang a song about an octopus.

As she turned into the administrative wing of the palace, she thought she caught sight of Adan. He was strolling down the hallway with a woman. A tall, dark-haired woman who had her arm looped in his. The woman laughed at something he said. They stopped and turned to face each other, and her heart lodged in her throat.

It was definitely Adan. He was so handsome in his white *dishdasha,* so exotic. She would know him anywhere.

He lifted his hand to the woman's face, stroked his fingers along her jaw while she smiled at him. And then he bent to kiss her on the cheek. Isabella's breath stopped in her chest as she watched him move his mouth to the woman's ear. Any second, he would kiss her on the mouth, whenever he ceased whispering whatever soft endearments he was whispering.

She couldn't look. She simply couldn't deal with having her heart ground beneath his custom loafers as she watched him kiss another woman, as she imagined him taking this woman to a bed with cool satin sheets and making love to her all afternoon long.

The way he'd made love to her not so long ago.

She'd been so stupid. So naive. She'd fallen for him. And, just like the last time, he didn't care one bit. His interest in her was tied to his desire to bed her. Once that was gone, so was he. Isabella whirled and fled back the way she'd come.

Adan spent the day in meetings with his cabinet, in phone calls with other heads of state and in going over the details for his coronation next week. He'd told Isabella he would be late, but he'd managed to finish earlier than he thought he would. Now he gathered the papers that Mahmoud had left for him and prepared to return to his private quarters.

He'd handled the situation badly this morning. But he hadn't known what to say. He hadn't known how to comfort her.

Everything he thought of saying sounded lame or trite. He was a man and a king, not a counselor. He understood action, not feelings. He understood how to make her body sing beneath his touch, but he didn't know how to soothe her soul.

He had to learn, however. If they were going to make this work—and he was determined they would for Rafiq's sake—he had to learn how to be a better husband.

The chef was preparing dinner when he arrived. He set the folder of papers down on a side table and followed the sound of voices to the courtyard. Rafiq was riding a toy car around the cobbled courtyard. Isabella sat at the table and clapped as he made his rounds.

She looked up as Adan stepped outside. The light in her eyes died—and then her gaze darted away. Inexplicably, a hard weight settled in his chest and refused to lift.

"We didn't expect you so early," she said.

"I didn't have as much to do as I thought."

"Of course," she replied, waving a hand airily. "You are your own boss, after all. If you wished to take an entire afternoon off, who would stop you?"

"Too many afternoons off and nothing would get done," he said mildly. "Though I expect things will settle into a predictable routine once the initial difficulties of transferring power to a new king are completed. My uncle never seemed to lack for family time, after all."

She pushed a lock of hair behind her ear. That glorious hair that he wanted to wrap his hands in as he made love to her in his bed. *Their* bed.

"And how was your day?" she asked. "Did anything interesting happen?"

"Interesting? Not especially."

She still hadn't looked at him. A tingle of alarm sounded in the back of his head.

She stood. "Well, I should take Rafiq for his bath."

He caught her wrist as she started to walk away. Her gaze fixed on his fingers where they encircled her.

"I'm sorry I'm not better at this," he said.

Her chin tilted up then. The full power of those green eyes turned on him—and he knew that something was wrong before she spoke.

"I remembered, Adan," she said softly. "I remembered what it was like. Our marriage, I mean."

His hand dropped away. He'd feared this even while he'd hoped for it. If she remembered, they could move forward. But if she remembered, she might not want to.

Right now he wasn't sure which side of the fence she'd come down on. Or why it mattered so damn much to him. She was still his wife, regardless. She couldn't do anything he didn't want her to do.

"When did this happen?" he asked, concentrating on the facts rather than the emotional impact.

"I had a headache this afternoon. I lay down for a while. It happened then."

Her voice sounded small, as if she were hurting so

much and trying to shrink from it. Guilt speared him. He had done that to her.

"Did you remember everything? The desert?"

She shook her head. "The doctor said I would probably never remember the days immediately before and after the accident." She swallowed. A laugh escaped her. Except that it wasn't really a laugh. "I still call it an accident," she said, "because I can't quite make myself name it what it is."

He blew out a rough breath. "It's not your fault, Isabella. Postnatal depression is a medical condition. There's no way of knowing who will get it and who won't."

He'd looked that up today when he'd had a chance. Aside from women with a history of depression in the family, one particular fact had leaped out at him: women who had stressful home lives and little or no support from their families were more susceptible than those who had more normal lives and relationships.

"It's terrifying to realize you weren't in control of yourself." She sucked in a breath. "I remembered when they handed him to me. I was overwhelmed, but not in a good way. He was like an alien to me, another being demanding my attention—someone else who wouldn't give me anything in return."

His throat hurt. He wanted to reach for her, but he didn't think she would appreciate it if he did. So he stood there with his hands hanging impotently at his sides.

"I suppose that shocks you," she said. "You'll think you were right to question my ability to be a good mother."

"I think you were overwhelmed by hormones. And by the fact you were alone."

She gave her head a tiny shake. "Women give birth alone all the time, Adan. Husbands go out of town on business or can't make it to the hospital in time. Those women don't have a problem bonding with their babies."

"I don't know what you want me to say to you."

"I don't think there's anything you can say," she replied.

"I can say I'm sorry."

Her head snapped up, her eyes flashing. "For what? For not being there? Or for not caring enough to notice something was wrong?" She ground her teeth together. Swore. "My father noticed, and look what he decided to do about it. Because he thought you would commit me, Adan. Even my father could see you didn't care about me."

He wanted to tell her she was wrong, of course he'd cared—but it wouldn't be the truth. He'd thought of his wife as another possession, someone who would be there to fill his bed, bear his children and run his household. He'd cared the way he would care about any living thing he was responsible for.

But that hadn't been enough. And he couldn't stand here and lie and say it was.

"I can't take back the past, Isabella. I can't change what happened."

A tear slipped down her cheek. She angrily swiped it away. "I saw you today, Adan."

He blinked. "You came to see me?"

"You were with a woman. You kissed her."

"I have kissed no woman but you," he said.

Rafiq kept zooming around the courtyard, squealing happily, but all Adan could see was the woman before him. The pain and anger on her face. The disenchantment.

"My God, you are unbelievable," she spat. "I saw you. And now I wonder if you lied to me at the Butterfly Palace, too. If you told me I was the only woman you'd been with in three years because you knew it would flatter me, make me more receptive—"

She broke off then, swallowed, and he knew she was fighting her tears.

"I did not lie, Isabella," he said stiffly. Fury whipped through him in waves. "I told you the truth because it *was* the truth. And you wanted me as much as I wanted you, regardless of how many women I might have slept with."

She stiffened as if he'd insulted her. "Well, you can rest assured that's not the case now. Because I don't want you anymore, Adan. I don't want you ever again."

CHAPTER THIRTEEN

HE was looking at her as if she'd grown two heads. But she'd been thinking a lot since she'd seen him with that woman today, and she'd come to a conclusion. She would not ever be pitiful again. She refused to love a man who couldn't love her, a man who cared so little about her that he could push her from his bed as easily as changing his shirt.

She was not a supplicant to the almighty King Adan ibn Najib Al Dhakir. She'd given up the job of supplication forever. She was the mother of his child, and she was going to be that for the rest of their lives.

But she would not live with him. She couldn't.

She loved him, and though it hurt her to imagine her life separate from him, she would not be a second thought to him—or anyone else—ever again.

"What do you want, then?" he asked, his jaw grinding.

He was annoyed, then. Good. Because she didn't need to be the only person affected, did she?

"A house nearby with a pool for Rafiq, and a small yard where he can play. It doesn't need to be anything grand."

"You want to live in a house near the palace?"

"Yes. And I want joint custody, Adan. I want Rafiq to know, starting right now, that I am his mother."

He'd gone slightly pale beneath his tan. Or maybe she'd just imagined it. "You want the divorce to proceed." It wasn't a question.

Her heart throbbed. Her breath sawed into her lungs painfully. "I think it's probably best. You've a wedding planned anyway. I assume the woman today was your bride-to-be."

He didn't answer at first. Then he nodded. "Jasmine. Yes."

Isabella was relieved that he was no longer denying he'd been with someone. At least he respected her enough to tell the truth now. Or maybe he just knew he'd been caught and saw no further need to prevaricate.

"How soon can this be done?" Because she couldn't stay here with him for a moment longer than she had to. She'd leave tonight if she could, but it was out of the question. Nothing could be accomplished that fast.

His brows drew down. She knew then that he'd got over the surprise and moved on to cold fury. Good, because she could deal with that better. If he were angry, she could be angry, too. It was far better than feeling hurt and love and sadness all at once.

"Do you truly want to do this to Rafiq?" he demanded. "Your parents were divorced, and you were torn between them."

She crossed her arms, as if it would somehow help to ward off the doubts that kept assailing her. "My mother went back to America. I'm not going anywhere. Besides, listening to them argue while they were still together didn't help much, either. It's better if we split, Adan, because there won't be any bitter feelings then. You can marry your new queen, and I can be our son's mother. When you have more children with her, you'll be grateful that I'm around to care for Rafiq."

"You've thought this all out, I see." His voice was so cold. So remote. If she touched him, would he feel like ice?

But no, she wasn't going to touch him. Not ever again. Her heart wept at the thought, but she stamped the feeling down deep. Rafiq was what mattered. She would endure what she had to for her son.

Seeing Adan with his new wife would kill her, but she would survive. In the long run, it would be better for her anyway. She could stop loving him and find someone who would really be good for her. Someone who loved her as much as she loved him.

And then, maybe, she would risk another child. If she knew her husband had her back no matter what happened, she would take the risk.

"I've had a lot of time to think today."

"Is this because of your memories? Or because of Jasmine?"

"It's everything, Adan. If you hadn't found me two weeks ago, we'd still be going on with our lives as they were. I'm grateful you found me, for Rafiq's sake, but everything else has been so hard to deal with. I don't think it does either of us any good to try and rebuild what was never really there in the first place."

He took a step closer to her then. Heat radiated from him in waves. "And what about the nights, Isabella? Can you so easily dismiss those, too?"

She moved a few steps away. He messed with her head, her heart, and she had to put distance between them or be pulled to him like filings to a magnet. She would be strong. She would not give in.

"The nights were amazing, Adan. You know that. And maybe they were necessary, in a way, though I don't know how you're going to explain them to your fiancée." She laughed then, the sound bordering on hysterical. "Of course you aren't going to explain them. Silly me. And she won't question you, because she's probably a perfect Jahfaran bride. Something I can never be again."

"You seem to know me so well," he said, his voice like ice chips pelting into her bruised heart. "Tell me— what else am I going to do? I'd like to know. It would make life so much easier."

"Don't make this any harder than it already is," she said.

"Why is it hard, Isabella? You've decreed this is the wisest, best outcome for everyone involved. So why is it difficult?"

Tears filled her eyes, made her vision swim. Damn it, she would *not* cry. "You know why," she declared. "I was starting to care for you again, Adan. But you've killed that, so don't worry that I'll change my mind. This is what's best for all of us. So divorce me and be done with it."

He looked so remote, so tall and handsome and regal as he stared at her with dark, glittering eyes. So alone. But he wasn't alone, not really. He never had been. She was the one who'd needed him, not the other way around.

But she was finished needing him. Whether it killed her or not, she was finished needing him.

"You have only to agree to it and we will be divorced."

Her heart stuttered in her chest. "Me? Why do I need to do anything?"

"Because we had a contract, Isabella, and I cannot set you aside without your agreement."

Her blood froze in her veins. "Is that why you took me to the Butterfly Palace? To get me to agree to a divorce?"

He bared his teeth in a cruel smile. "Precisely."

She could only gape at him. When she'd thought of a divorce as something only he could do, she'd felt as if it was out of her hands. As if there was nothing she could do or say to either proceed with or prevent it from happening. In a way, that had been a comfort.

But now? Now the responsibility was hers. The dissolution of their marriage lay on her shoulders. With a simple yes, the process would begin.

"You are despicable," she growled. "You didn't want to give me time with our son because it was the right thing to do. You wanted me to fail, and you wanted me to agree to divorce you once I had."

A muscle in his jaw ticked. "That was my intention, yes."

"And if it didn't happen the way you thought? What then?"

"Your agreement was meant to speed up the process. It would not have prevented it."

She could only stare at him, her heart breaking again and again. "And then you slept with me. My God, how could you do it? How could you be so cruel?"

"It wasn't my intention. It just happened."

She would have walked over and slapped him if not for their son still happily playing in the courtyard.

She would never, ever let her child see how much she despised his father at that moment.

"But I changed my mind about divorcing you, Isabella," he said. "Does that count for anything in this perfect little world you've devised?"

A tear spilled down her cheek in spite of her wish not to cry in front of him. He looked anguished, but she shook her head, certain it was a trick of her blurry vision. "No, not really. Because I'm sure it was for logical reasons that had nothing to do with what was best for me, and everything to do with what you thought best for you and Rafiq."

He swore softly in Arabic then. "You don't think much of me, do you?"

"Does it matter what I think, Adan? Do you really care?"

"Tell me you want the divorce, Isabella. Tell me, and it will be done."

She sucked in a trembling breath. Bowed her head. Swore six ways to Sunday that she wouldn't cry. That she would be strong and do this. "Yes," she managed. "I want a divorce."

He stood very, very still. And then he said, so quietly that she had to strain to hear it, "Then it will be done."

It took another two days before the papers were in his hands. Adan stared at the legal documents the solicitor had sent over, the words flowing together as nonsensically as if they were written in another language. He blinked, focused, and they coalesced again.

Divorce.

It was all there. All he had to do was sign it and then

have it sent to Isabella for her signature. They would no longer be married, and he could proceed with the wedding to Jasmine.

Except that he'd spoken with Jasmine two days ago when she'd come to the palace and told her that he'd decided not to divorce Isabella after all. She'd seemed so happy for him, smiling and giving him a big hug.

"I knew it would work out."

"You were right, as always," he'd said. And then he'd walked her down the hall to the entry, where he'd given her a kiss on the cheek and told her that she was a very special woman who deserved to find love rather than marry an old friend in order to help him out.

He'd said those words to her, but now, if he granted Isabella's wish, he would have to ask for Jasmine's help once more. At least until he was crowned next week.

He threw down the pen that he'd been holding. It had hovered over the line requiring his signature, but he'd been unable to form the words.

He wanted Isabella, and not simply because it would be easier.

He didn't want Jasmine, or any other woman. He wanted his wife. The woman who'd given him a son.

He wanted the woman he loved. Adan propped his elbows on the desk and put his head in his hands. He deserved everything that had happened.

Because as he'd stood there listening to her calmly telling him she didn't want him, that she wanted to live separately from him because he'd killed whatever feelings she'd had for him, he'd realized that his skin felt as if it had been turned inside out so that all his nerves were exposed. His heart pounded in his head, his throat, his stomach, until he felt sick with the throbbing, until he realized why it wasn't going away.

Why it would never go away.

He was in love with his wife. He'd wanted nothing more than to gather her to him and hold her tight, to tell her he loved her not only with words, but also with his body, with every breath he ever took.

But she hated him. In that moment, she hated him, and he'd known there was nothing he could do about it.

He deserved it. He'd taken her for granted when they'd wed. He'd ignored her, discounted her and failed her when she'd needed him the most. He didn't deserve her love then or now.

So he'd stood there and let her censure rain down on him. And when the first lone tear slid down her cheek, he'd hated himself for making her cry. He'd given her the truth because it was the only thing she'd wanted from him then, though it hurt her and made her think worse of him than she already did.

Adan shoved back from the desk and snatched up the divorce papers. He would not be a coward. He would give her what she wanted. But he wasn't going to be the first one to sign.

He strode out of his office, ignoring Mahmoud's surprised expression. There was an ambassador waiting, and a trade agreement on the line, but he didn't care right now. He would fix everything later. First he had to see Isabella.

He stalked down the hallway, took a shortcut through another wing to the royal apartments and burst through the door. He knew he would find her here because he'd not yet managed to locate a suitable house in town.

In truth, he hadn't tried very hard. He would, but he just hadn't wanted to let her go yet.

She shot to her feet as he entered her room without knocking. She was dressed in a pair of her Hawaiian shorts and a tank top, and his groin tightened at the display of so much gorgeous skin. Skin he wanted to worship.

Her hair was wild, as always. God, how he loved her hair. It suited her so much more than the sleek, false style she'd once worn to please him ever had.

She looked vulnerable, but then her expression hardened as she crossed her arms and leveled him with a green stare.

"Since when is it okay to burst into someone's room without knocking?"

He thrust the papers at her. "I've brought you something," he said, keeping his anguish tightly leashed. His voice sounded hard, cold, but he couldn't help it. It was the only way he could do this.

She held out her hand and took the papers. When she looked up at him again, her eyes were huge in her face. A tiny flame of hope kindled in his belly. He snuffed it out again. He would not seek hope where there was none.

She hated him. She would be glad to be rid of him. But she was going to sign first. She would be the one who ended it, not him.

"What am I supposed to do with this?" she asked. She bit her bottom lip and he nearly groaned.

"Sign it. It's what you wanted."

She looked down at the papers in her hand again. "You haven't signed."

"You first."

She walked over to a table and laid the papers down, smoothing them. "I need a pen," she said, not looking at him.

He growled as he spun and went into another room. He snatched a pen from a desk in the living area, then returned and held it out to her.

She hesitated, but then took it. Their skin brushed and he felt the jolt to his toes.

She uncapped the pen, then poised it over the paper. He could see her chest rising and falling, could see how the tempo increased as she stood there, hesitating.

Then the pen touched the paper. With a growl, he snatched the documents away. She squeaked as he ripped them in two.

Then he tossed them on the floor and grabbed her by the arms. "I don't want this," he said. The words felt as if they'd been ripped from his chest. "I don't deserve you, I know I don't—but I want you, Isabella. I need you."

She blinked. And then she shuddered in his grip. "I can't do this, Adan. Please don't keep touching me."

"I know you hate me. I know I deserve it. But give me a chance, Isabella. Give me a chance…"

A sob burst from her then and he let her go, though it tore him apart to do so. But he couldn't cause her any more pain than he already had.

"Why are you doing this?" she asked. "Why can't you just let me go?"

"I love you," he said, his throat aching with the words. "I can't let you go because I love you."

She sagged against the arm of the couch and buried her face in her hands. And then she was sobbing uncontrollably, her shoulders shaking, her tears like knife thrusts to his heart.

"I'm sorry," he said, tears welling in his eyes. "I'm sorry. I'll go. I'll get another set of papers and I will sign them. I will let you go, Isabella, if it's what you want."

He turned blindly. He had to get out of there before he did something stupid, like sink to his knees and beg.

"Adan," she said, and he stopped. "I'm scared."

And that was it, the moment of surrender. Hope blossomed inside again, but this time it wouldn't be crushed. He crossed to her as she straightened, and then he was holding her tight, his fists curled in her hair as he bent his head to inhale her scent.

"I'm scared, too," he admitted. "I never expected to feel this way."

She slipped her arms around his waist and squeezed him tight. "It'll be all right. It has to be all right if we're both scared."

He tilted her head back and gazed down into her glorious eyes. "I'm sorry for all the pain I've ever caused you, *habibti*. I'll do everything in my power to make it up to you, I swear. One day, you will fall in love with me again. And then I will deserve it."

She smiled through her tears. "My God, for a man who bears the responsibility for an entire nation, you certainly are dense."

He searched her gaze—and then he saw it. Love, shining through for him. His heart soared. "You love me," he said in wonder.

"Yes," she said simply. "I do."

"I want to question this good fortune," he said, "but I will not. I'm never giving you a reason to think twice about why you love me."

And then, to make sure she couldn't think at all, he took her to bed and spent the rest of the afternoon making sure she knew how thoroughly he loved every inch of her—body and soul.

the tent, she saw three camels waiting for the trip back to the civilization she'd left a week earlier, returning alone. She knew how they'd feel about that.

In her own body, no one ever—

EPILOGUE

ISABELLA rolled over in the blankets and discovered she was alone. She opened her eyes and stretched languorously. Just then, the tent flap drew back and a man in traditional garb entered.

"Well, hello, my desert lord and master," she purred. "Where have you been?"

Adan came over to where she lay on the king-size bed that occupied center stage in the tent. Lush pillows were piled around her, and a thick coverlet hid her body from view.

His fingers caught the edge of the cover and began to ease it down.

"This is not just a pleasure trip, my love," he said. "Some of us have work to do."

"Mmm, thankfully, not me."

He bent and took her mouth. She wrapped her arms around his neck and arched up into him as he uncovered her breasts.

"You are very naughty, Your Majesty," he said. "And very spoiled."

"But you love me."

"I do. Utterly and completely." He kissed her again,

and then ripped the covers from her naked body. A shiver of anticipation tingled through her.

"Now get up, Your Laziness. The day awaits us."

Isabella pouted. "Get up? Since when does the great King Adan ibn Najib Al Dhakir gaze upon his wife's naked body and not want sex?"

"Oh, he definitely wants it," he purred. "But I have a meeting with tribal chieftains to attend. Later, I will remember this conversation and make you pay accordingly."

Isabella laughed. "Make me pay? Who's the naughty one now, Adan?"

His eyes were hot. "We'll have to find that out, won't we?"

She reached for her robe and slipped it on as she stepped from the bed. Then she went into his arms.

"I like the way you think," she said before she gave him a long, lingering kiss.

"You make me want to be late," he said when she pulled back.

"It's not good form to be late."

He laughed. "You are not only naughty, you're also a tease."

"I'm building suspense for later," she said, grinning. "Have you seen the children this morning?"

"Rafiq wants to go horseback-riding. Little Kalila wants to know when we can go home—because the sand, she informs me, gets into everything. And the twins want to swim in the sea."

Isabella sighed. "Then I had better get dressed, hadn't I?"

He gave her a smack on the rear. "This is what I have

said, *habibti*." Then he kissed her again, swiftly. "But tonight you are mine."

"With pleasure, my lord."

"That is certainly my intention," he purred. He had reached the tent flap when he stopped and shook his head. Then he turned around and stalked back over to her.

"I'm the king," he said, slipping the robe from her shoulders. "I can be late if I want."

Isabella laughed. "I do love a man who knows what he wants. And who will do anything to get it."

Like flying halfway around the world to collect his runaway wife. Like ripping up divorce papers before she could sign them. Like this, now, when he showed her once more with words and caresses just how much he adored her.

Oh, yes, there was something to be said for a man who knew what he wanted.

* * * * *

CLASSIC

REQUEST YOUR FREE BOOKS!

2 FREE NOVELS PLUS
2 FREE GIFTS!

YES! Please send me 2 FREE Harlequin Presents® novels and my 2 FREE gifts (gifts are worth about $10). After receiving them, if I don't wish to receive any more books, I can return the shipping statement marked "cancel." If I don't cancel, I will receive 6 brand-new novels every month and be billed just $4.30 per book in the U.S. or $4.99 per book in Canada. That's a saving of at least 14% off the cover price! It's quite a bargain! Shipping and handling is just 50¢ per book in the U.S. and 75¢ per book in Canada.* I understand that accepting the 2 free books and gifts places me under no obligation to buy anything. I can always return a shipment and cancel at any time. Even if I never buy another book, the two free books and gifts are mine to keep forever.

106/306 HDN FERQ

Name		
	(PLEASE PRINT)	

Address		
		Apt. #

City	State/Prov.	Zip/Postal Code

Signature (if under 18, a parent or guardian must sign)

Mail to the Reader Service:
IN U.S.A.: P.O. Box 1867, Buffalo, NY 14240-1867
IN CANADA: P.O. Box 609, Fort Erie, Ontario L2A 5X3

Not valid for current subscribers to Harlequin Presents books.

**Are you a current subscriber to Harlequin Presents books
and want to receive the larger-print edition?
Call 1-800-873-8635 or visit www.ReaderService.com.**

* Terms and prices subject to change without notice. Prices do not include applicable taxes. Sales tax applicable in N.Y. Canadian residents will be charged applicable taxes. Offer not valid in Quebec. This offer is limited to one order per household. All orders subject to credit approval. Credit or debit balances in a customer's account(s) may be offset by any other outstanding balance owed by or to the customer. Please allow 4 to 6 weeks for delivery. Offer available while quantities last.

Your Privacy—The Reader Service is committed to protecting your privacy. Our Privacy Policy is available online at www.ReaderService.com or upon request from the Reader Service.

We make a portion of our mailing list available to reputable third parties that offer products we believe may interest you. If you prefer that we not exchange your name with third parties, or if you wish to clarify or modify your communication preferences, please visit us at www.ReaderService.com/consumerschoice or write to us at Reader Service Preference Service, P.O. Box 9062, Buffalo, NY 14269. Include your complete name and address.

HPI1B

Get swept away with a brand-new miniseries
by USA TODAY bestselling author

MARGARET WAY

The Langdon Dynasty

Amelia Norton knows that in order to embrace her future,
she must first face her past. As she unravels her family's secrets,
she is forced to turn to gorgeous cattleman Dev Langdon for
support—the man she vowed never to fall for again.

Against the haze of the sweltering Australian heat Mel's
guarded exterior begins to crumble...and Dev will do
whatever it takes to convince his childhood sweetheart
to be his bride.

THE CATTLE KING'S BRIDE

Available April 2012

And look for

ARGENTINIAN IN THE OUTBACK

Coming in May 2012

Taft Bowman knew he'd ruined any chance he'd had for happiness with Laura Pendleton when he drove her away years ago...and into the arms of another man, thousands of miles away. Now she was back, a widow with two small children...and despite himself, he was starting to believe in second chances.

Harlequin Special® Edition® presents a new installment in USA TODAY *bestselling author* RaeAnne Thayne's *miniseries,* THE COWBOYS OF COLD CREEK.

Enjoy a sneak peek of A COLD CREEK REUNION

Available April 2012 from Harlequin® Special Edition®

A younger woman stood there, and from this distance he had only a strange impression, as though she was somehow standing on an island of calm amid the chaos of the scene, the flashing lights of the emergency vehicles, shouts between his crew members, the excited buzz of the crowd.

And then the woman turned and he just about tripped over a snaking fire hose somebody shouldn't have left there.

Laura.

He froze, and for the first time in fifteen years as a firefighter, he forgot about the incident, his mission, just what the hell he was doing here.

Laura.

Ten years. He hadn't seen her in all that time, since the week before their wedding when she had given him back his ring and left town. Not just town. She had left the whole damn country, as if she couldn't run far enough to get away from him.

Some part of him desperately wanted to think he had made some kind of mistake. It couldn't be her. That was just some other slender woman with a long sweep of honey-blond hair and big, blue, unforgettable eyes. But no. It was definitely Laura. Sweet and lovely.

Not his.

He was going to have to go over there and talk to her. He didn't want to. He wanted to stand there and pretend he hadn't seen her. But he was the fire chief. He couldn't hide out just because he had a painful history with the daughter of the property owner.

Sometimes he hated his job.

Will Taft and Laura be able to make the years recede...or is the gulf between them too broad to ever cross?

Find out in
A COLD CREEK REUNION
Available April 2012 from Harlequin® Special Edition®
wherever books are sold.

Celebrate the 30th anniversary
of Harlequin® Special Edition® with a bonus story
included in each Special Edition® book in April!

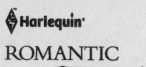

ROMANTIC
SUSPENSE

Danger is hot on their heels!

Catch the thrill with author

LINDA CONRAD

Chance, Texas

Sam Chance, a U.S. marshal in the Witness Security
Service, is sworn to protect Grace Brown and her
one-year-old son after Grace testifies against an infamous
drug lord and he swears revenge. With Grace on the edge of
fleeing, Sam knows there is only one safe place he can take
her—home. But when the danger draws near, it's not just
Sam's life on the line but his heart, too.

Watch out for

Texas Baby Sanctuary
Available April 2012

Texas Manhunt
Available May 2012

Harlequin Blaze™
red-hot reads

**Sizzling fairy tales
to make every fantasy come true!**

Fan-favorite authors
Tori Carrington and Kate Hoffmann
bring readers

Blazing Bedtime Stories, Volume VI

MAID FOR HIM...

Successful businessman Kieran Morrison doesn't dare hope for
a big catch when he goes fishing. But when he wakes up one
night to find a beautiful woman seemingly unconscious on the
deck of his sailboat, he lands one bigger than he could ever
have imagined by way of mermaid Daphne Moore.
But is she real? Or just a fantasy?

OFF THE BEATEN PATH

Greta Adler and Alex Hansen have been friends for seven years.
So when Greta agrees to accompany Alex at a mountain retreat
owned by a client, she doesn't realize that Alex has a different
path he wants their relationshiop to take.
But will Greta follow his lead?

Available April 2012 wherever books are sold.

www.Harlequin.com

HB79679